PLAYING BY HEART

Teresa's eyes were mostly closed, and her body moved with the fluid melody. A small smile rested on her lips, and her pale face glowed with the love of the music she was creating. Richard watched, enthralled with her beauty, slowly losing himself as well. Her calm and the beautiful music filled him with peace.

He sat forward in his chair, ready to turn the page, when she reached across him for a key at the far end of the keyboard. With the feel of her body's heat, even momentarily against his, he was forcibly reminded once again that this was their wedding night.

He wondered what she was expecting. He had promised not to touch her, but would he, could he, hold himself to that promise? Her scent and the warmth that radiated from her body reminded him of a field of lavender in summer.

He had not realized how difficult it was going to be to know that she was his wife and yet he could not touch her. He felt the tension in his body mount. Let him just make it through this evening. Perhaps it would get easier after that.

BOOK YOUR PLACE ON OUR WEBSITE AND MAKE THE READING CONNECTION!

We've created a customized website just for our very special readers, where you can get the inside scoop on everything that's going on with Zebra, Pinnacle and Kensington books.

When you come online, you'll have the exciting opportunity to:

- View covers of upcoming books
- Read sample chapters
- Learn about our future publishing schedule (listed by publication month *and author*)
- Find out when your favorite authors will be visiting a city near you
- Search for and order backlist books from our online catalog
- Check out author bios and background information
- Send e-mail to your favorite authors
- Meet the Kensington staff online
- Join us in weekly chats with authors, readers and other guests
- Get writing guidelines
- AND MUCH MORE!

**Visit our website at
http://www.kensingtonbooks.com**

Miss Seton's Sonata

Meredith Bond

ZEBRA BOOKS
Kensington Publishing Corp.
http://www.kensingtonbooks.com

This book would not have happened without the loving support and brutal honesty of my husband and the reluctant patience and support of my two children, Robin and Anjali.

ZEBRA BOOKS are published by

Kensington Publishing Corp.
850 Third Avenue
New York, NY 10022

All Kensington titles, imprints and distributed lines are available at special quantity discounts for bulk purchases for sales promotion, premiums, fund-raising, educational or institutional use.

Special book excerpts or customized printings can also be created to fit specific needs. For details, write or phone the office of the Kensington Special Sales Manager: Kensington Publishing Corp., 850 Third Avenue, New York, NY 10022. Attn. Special Sales Department. Phone: 1-800-221-2647.

Zebra and the Z logo Reg. U.S. Pat. & TM Off.

First Printing: January 2004
10 9 8 7 6 5 4 3 2 1

Printed in the United States of America

One

Richard heard the beautiful music and felt all of his muscles tense. His ghosts were back.

As he stepped into his desolate house, he thought that the fog outside had penetrated his mind. The shadows cast by the single candle flickering on the dusty table somehow accentuated the gloom. He stopped and listened, his coat and hat slipping from his fingers onto the floor.

Surely he was imagining the music? He had to be. He shuddered involuntarily. The only people who had ever played music in this house had been his sister and his wife. But they were both dead.

Their ghosts still haunted his imagination, it was true, but he had never actually heard them playing music. Beethoven's Fourteenth Sonata had been his wife's favorite. How she had loved the sweet, soft melody! Today, however, the music echoing through the empty town house sounded eerie.

Richard swallowed hard. In the mist of his mind's eye he saw Julia smiling and playing her music. She was there, beckoning to him, with her light brown hair pulled up, leaving only tendrils curling lightly about her face and neck. Her soft green eyes were laughing at him, loving him. His senses were flooded with the tantalizing scent of roses, which she had always worn. Her voice called to him through the music she played. It moved him toward her, ever closer.

He found himself just outside the music room, his hand on the door handle. He stood there, staring at the narrow strip of light spilling out from under the door. He had not been inside this room since she died. He was not sure he wanted to go in now.

No, he could not do it. He just could not open the door. Although he knew that the ghosts were only in his imagination, the music seemed so very real. And, for once in his life, Richard Angles, the intrepid Marquis of Merrick, knew he was truly frightened.

Richard squared his shoulders. He would prove to himself that the music was not there, that *she* was not there. Taking a deep breath, he flung open the door so hard that it banged into the wall.

The music stopped. Richard blinked, his eyes adjusting to the brightness of the room. As he focused on the grand pianoforte in the corner, he let out his breath. There was someone there, but it was not Julia. The girl sitting at the pianoforte had black hair and eyes, and her face was alabaster white, with deep pink lips.

His relief and wonder was suddenly transformed into overpowering rage. Who had dared to play such a trick on him?

"Who are you? What are you doing here?" he demanded in his most stern, masterful baritone.

The girl stood up so quickly that the gilt chair she had been sitting on fell to the floor with a loud crash.

She stood for a moment looking him over from head to toe. He watched as the emotions in her marvelously expressive eyes changed quickly from alarm and shock to assessment and then to flashing pride. "I am Teresa Seton. I am staying next door with my aunt, Lady Swinborne. The housekeeper has given me permission to be here. She said his lordship was away from home, and that I might practice on his pianoforte." Her small chin rose a fraction of an inch. "Who are you?"

As her eyes raked down his body, Richard was immediately made aware of his inappropriate attire. He was dressed in one of his most threadbare coats, at least three, if not four, years out-of-date. His boots were scuffed and well worn, and his breeches clearly had seen better days.

He assessed the situation, his anger fading quickly. If she were indeed Lady Swinborne's niece, then judging from her age, which could not have been more than eighteen or nineteen, that meant only one thing. She was in London to make her come-out. And, if that were so, Richard wanted nothing less than for it to be made known that he was in town. He knew the ways of matchmaking mamas—or aunts.

He made up his mind quickly. As Teresa Seton clearly had no idea who he was, he saw no reason to enlighten her about his identity. Yet, he did want to hear that music again. It was a need deep inside him that he had not realized existed until the music had stopped.

He stepped farther into the room, deliberately slumping his broad shoulders a little and making his voice sound as contrite and timid as he could manage without losing face altogether. "My name is Richard. I, ah, look after the house." That was honest enough. He hated lying outright, but by leaving out the details, he could get by without revealing who he was. "I am sorry to disturb you. I was not told that anyone was here. Could I . . . do you think I could listen to you play a little? It was very beautiful."

The girl looked at him, a little confused and evidently taken aback by this sudden change in his demeanor. Then, shrugging her shoulders in that very continental gesture, she turned around to right her chair, saying, "Yes, of course. I do not mind if you listen."

She went back to the Beethoven sonata she had been playing but kept a wary eye on Richard. He came farther into the room and sat down gingerly on the edge of one of the chairs arranged in neat rows in front of the pianoforte, trying to give the impression that he wasn't sure if he was allowed to sit there. But very soon he realized that she was completely taken up by the music and was paying him no attention.

As Miss Seton lost herself in the music, she seemed to change as well. Richard watched her body sway with the music as she played the flowing notes, and she took on the same ethereal quality as the music. She had a glowing luminosity that was amazing, enticing. It was as if the pianoforte and the girl were one instrument, developed for the sole purpose of creating the shimmering brilliance of the sonata.

Richard smiled to himself at his fanciful imaginings, but he could not deny that there was something remarkable about her. As she played, she moved with grace, her head tilted slightly sideways, her eyes mostly closed. Her black eyelashes were long, providing a striking contrast to the pale cheeks on which they lay. To add to her ghostly quality, she was dressed in a white gown with full long sleeves. A faint print of light pink flowers and a pink ribbon around the high waist of the dress were the only touches of color present.

The music slowed and then faded away as Miss Seton gently touched the last lingering notes of the piece. Her dark eyes slowly opened and met his. For a moment neither of them moved, just let the last of the notes slowly evaporate into the silence of the room.

She broke the contact, quickly turning back to the pianoforte. Toying with some music in front of her, turning over pages, she silently prepared to play the next piece. This one she clearly did not know as well and had to play from the score. Richard did not recognize the piece, but the sound was still soft and lilting.

She was really superb at the pianoforte. Richard closed his eyes and sat back in his chair, letting the music carry him away. The graceful melody was calming, and filled him with a sense of his long-lost happiness.

A pause in the flowing music brought him back into the room with a jolt. He opened his eyes to see Miss Seton struggling with the sheets of music, trying to turn the page. He jumped up and helped her straighten it out, then stayed standing next to her so that he could turn the pages for her.

As she reached for a key directly in front of him, her arm accidentally brushed against his leg. Although it was the briefest of touches, it seemed to leave a trail of heat on his thigh. With a shock he found himself fighting an intense desire to lean closer to her, to feel the touch of her skin. His heart was pounding, and parts of him were tingling in ways he had not thought to feel again for a long time.

Guilt stabbed at him at his body's betrayal of the loving memory of his wife. Taking a deep breath, he forced himself to step back. As he did so, however, he wondered whether she, too, was aware of him. Since he had moved closer to her, she had begun playing self-consciously, not allowing the music to fully take over her whole body as she had before.

He had to make himself concentrate on the pages of music in front of them. He noticed that Miss Seton had reached the end of the page, and he reached out to turn it so that she would not need to pause in her playing.

She did stop, however, and looked up at him with her dark eyebrows raised.

"You know how to read music?"

Richard was caught off guard. Naturally, he, the Marquis of Merrick, knew how to read music. But would someone who was only a steward? No, of course not. What a fool he was to be caught out in his lie so quickly.

"I, ah, yes. My mother played the pianoforte, and she taught me when I was young." Let her make of that what she will, Richard thought defiantly.

Richard had hoped that this terse explanation would leave Miss Seton no other choice than to accept what he said and to resume playing. But she continued her searching look. Perhaps she was trying to figure out exactly who he was, or perhaps she simply felt the same sort of warmth he was feeling now as he stood so close to her.

She nodded her head, finally accepting his explanation. "Bring another chair forward so you do not have to stand," she directed him.

Although the marquis in him bristled at her calmly commanding manner, he did as he was told. Once he had settled himself, Miss Seton went back to playing. He turned the pages of music as she played and let the music and her faint lavender scent wash over him.

Miss Seton had been playing a faster piece, and Richard had found himself nodding to the rhythm. As he reached for the sheet of music to turn it, the clock in the hall began to strike the hour. Miss Seton stopped playing with a start and began to count. "Five! My aunt will be furious if I am late!"

Jumping up, she fled for the door. But before running out, she hesitated, then turned to him. Her pale face broke into a soft smile. "Thank you, ah, Richard."

Richard had instinctively risen. "My pleasure. When

will I see . . ." His sentence was left unfinished as he realized that she was already gone. As he sat back into his chair, he was surprised to find that he was smiling. He also realized that for the first time since Julia had left him, he looked forward to tomorrow.

TWO

Teresa sat alone in the corner of Lady Jersey's large white-and-gold drawing room the next afternoon. Although the decor much too opulent for her own tastes, Teresa had to admit that it was an impressive room. She bent her head to focus on her hands tightly clenched in her lap as the gay sound of trilling feminine chatter resounded all around her. Why, she thought miserably, did Aunt Catherine have to drag her out to pay morning calls?

Of course, Sally Jersey was a great friend of her aunt's. She also happened to be one of the most powerful women of the *ton*. If Teresa were to say something inappropriate in front of her, it could seriously undermine her social reputation. Not that she had much of one yet, she thought ruefully, but she had been in London for only a month and her aunt had said that she was still hopeful that Teresa would come out of her shell.

Teresa was not as confident, but at the moment she was much more afraid that, were she to say anything, she would only succeed in embarrassing herself. She always did. She was much too outspoken. But she was determined not to let that happen today.

As she listened silently to the flow of conversation around her, her attention was caught by the exchange between two girls about her own age. They sat on a set-

tee not too far away. One, whom Teresa recognized as a
Diamond of the first water, had mahogany-colored hair,
with delicate curls emphasizing her long neck. Her eyes
were a delightful green and her complexion was flaw-
less. Teresa discreetly leaned to the side to catch a
glimpse of her companion. Although unfashionably
blond, she was also very pretty, Teresa thought, with her
peaches-and-cream complexion and pale blue eyes.
With her own black hair, black eyes, and ghastly white
skin, Teresa thought ruefully that she was like an ugly
duckling among the swans.

Teresa watched the conversation unfold. It was not
actually much of an exchange. Rather, the Diamond
seemed to be lecturing the other young lady.

"You know, my dear Miss Peyton, with your dowry
you really ought to make more of an effort to put yourself forward. This shrinking demeanor of yours is not
destined to attract the more eligible gentlemen," she
said with an air of authority.

Miss Peyton looked wide-eyed at her mentor, nodding in agreement. Yet Teresa noticed worry lines
appear on the young lady's broad forehead. "I am certain that you are correct, Miss Bowden-Smyth. I will
certainly try. . . ."

"You must not only try, you must succeed—else it is
certain that your papa's expenditures for this season will
be as good as forfeit. And from what I understand, he
can little afford to waste such moneys as he is undoubt-
edly spending on your wardrobe." The Diamond looked
over her companion in an exaggerated fashion and then
sniffed, "It is so unfortunate that you were not blessed,
as I was, with prettier coloring. However, you do seem
to be doing the best with what you have."

If it was at all possible for someone to appear to
shrink into oneself while still sitting straight, Miss Pey-

ton managed to do it. Teresa barely kept herself from gasping with outrage at the Diamond's cruel words. She could take no more of this harangue. If Miss Peyton would not stand up for herself, certainly there was something that she, Teresa, could do to defend the poor girl.

Teresa moved her chair a little closer to Miss Peyton.

"I am so sorry to interrupt your conversation," Teresa began, smiling brightly at Miss Peyton, "but did I not see you dancing last night at Lady Arundell's ball with Lord Millhaven?" Teresa deliberately named the most sought-after bachelor of the season.

Miss Peyton colored slightly. "Y-yes," the girl stammered. "His lordship was kind enough to lead me out for the quadrille."

Teresa nodded her head knowingly. "Yes, I thought I remembered you. I am Teresa Seton. I am staying with my aunt, Lady Swinborne, for the season." She gestured over to her aunt, who was deep in conversation with Princess Esterhazy, one of the patronesses of Almacks.

The Diamond and Miss Peyton followed the direction of Teresa's hand and were clearly impressed with her connections. This did not, however, stop the Diamond from looking Teresa over as if she were sizing up the competition.

"Were you at Lady Arundell's ball? I do not remember seeing you," she said, raising one side of her lips in a slight sneer. Teresa's temper rose slightly as she grasped that she had been weighed and found to be lacking.

"Oh, no? Well, it was such a crush, was it not?" Teresa said, deliberately ignoring the implied slight. In truth, she had not been seen because she had managed to hide among the potted palms for much of the evening. She knew she was even worse than Miss Peyton when it came to putting herself forward.

"Indeed," said Miss Peyton, leaning closer to Teresa as she spoke. Clearly, she felt better about herself ever since Teresa had mentioned her dance with Lord Millhaven. "Did you happen to see Lord Byron? I saw him when he first came in. Is he not the most handsome gentleman?" she gushed.

The Diamond was on home territory here. She smoothed some nonexistent wrinkles from her dress. "Lord Byron is a personal acquaintance of mine."

"Is he?" Miss Peyton said, awe written on her face.

The biscuit in Teresa's hand broke between her fingers with an audible snap. Making herself smile as sweetly as she could, she said, "One cannot deny that he is a handsome gentleman, but I believe him to be quite ridiculous with his romantic airs and his sloe eyes. Why, it quite makes me laugh every time I see him. And the way the young ladies of the *ton* throw themselves at him is appalling!"

Encouraged by Miss Peyton's open expression, Teresa leaned forward conspiratorially. "I do believe that he encourages the advances of these silly females just to puff up his own self-worth. Why, I even heard that some brazen-faced girl actually swooned in his arms last night!"

The face of the Diamond blanched, and then turned a deep red. In a constricted tone of voice she said, "I was . . . I was overcome by the heat in the room."

She immediately got up, and moved away from Teresa as quickly as was possible in the crowded drawing room.

Miss Peyton watched the Diamond's retreating back. Then, giving Teresa a rather apologetic look, she, too, got up, and hurried after her companion, who was already conversing with a newcomer. Teresa watched Miss Peyton nodding in agreement as the Diamond, with a sneer on her face, whispered confidences to her friend. The way Miss Peyton kept looking back at her clearly told Teresa that she was the subject of the Diamond's gossip.

Teresa realized with chagrin that she had just made an enemy of someone who had the power to make her entrance into society much more difficult. Why had she not listened to her own good counsel and kept her mouth shut? Yet, surely she could not have sat by idly while Miss Peyton was being so thoroughly browbeaten by her companion! She shook her head, smiling a little to herself. In any case, it had felt good to discomfit that supercilious nonpareil, if only for a moment.

She did, however, want to go home before she committed any more *faux pas*. Where was Aunt Catherine? She spied her deep in conversation with Lady Jersey. There was no way Teresa was going to get her attention, let alone convince her to leave.

Teresa slumped down in her chair, but then immediately heard her mother's voice in her head reprimanding her to sit up straight. She sighed, straightened, and then let her mind wander to someplace she would rather be.

She wished she could return to Lord Merrick's house to practice her music. The familiarity of the ivory keys under her fingers the day before had made her feel at home for the first time since she had come to this utterly foreign place. She knew in her heart that Lord Merrick's music room would become her haven amid the many trials she would face in London.

A picture of Richard intruded abruptly. That was surprising. Since she had left Lord Merrick's house the previous day, she had not thought of the gentleman she had met there, but now that she had a moment for quiet reflection, she wondered exactly who he was.

Remembering the way he carried himself, and the way he spoke, she quickly decided that he was indeed a gentleman. He must be some poor relation of Lord Merrick's, hired by the marquis to look after his home while he was gone. That was the only plausible explanation of why he had, at first, been so angry at finding her there. And also, he could read music. Clearly, he had to have been wellborn to learn such a thing. Perhaps his family had lost its money through some improvident investments, or, as was more likely, through gambling.

Teresa shook her head. It was quite sad how people could ruin the lives of their children through the turn of a card. She hoped she would see the gentleman again. He had been kind to her, and his presence had been very comforting somehow. She felt herself get warm as she remembered her accidental brush with his leg and how her heart had hammered after that. She had been so embarrassed that only instinct had let her carry on playing her music. He, too, had seemed discomforted by it. She was grateful that he had stepped away from her.

She took a deep breath to compose herself, and looked up from her woolgathering just in time to see her aunt and Lady Jersey bearing down on her. Lady Swinborne's normally stern face was flushed with pleasure. Although time had not been so kind to the lady's figure, her face was still remarkably young, with few wrinkles, and her brown hair was only lightly salted with gray. Her choice of deep, sober colors did a good job of hiding her increasing bulk, but it was her height that allowed her to maintain an almost regal air.

"Teresa, Lady Jersey has come up with the most wonderful idea!"

Teresa's heart sank. This could be nothing that she

would enjoy. She curved her lips upward into a smile that, she hoped, would come across as joyful expectation. "Yes, Aunt Catherine?"

"You are in for a rare treat. Lady Jersey is going to take you to her own *modiste!*"

Teresa's breath caught in her throat. She was to go shopping with Lady Jersey? Having such an esteemed member of society take a personal interest in her was a huge stroke of good fortune. And yet a voice inside her head screamed in horror. She was going to be alone with Lady Jersey for an afternoon. An entire afternoon, where any misspoken word could lead to a major *faux pas* and ruin any future she might have among the *ton*. The thought terrified her.

Teresa struggled to control her panic. She owed it to herself to make the most of this opportunity. In the steadiest voice she could muster, she said, "I can barely believe the great honor that you are bestowing upon me, Lady Jersey. It is too good of you."

Lady Jersey patted her shoulder. "Not at all, my dear girl. Your aunt and I have been friends since our own come-out. It is the least I could do for a true friend like Catherine. I had always hoped to be able to do such a service for a child of Catherine's. Alas, it was not to be. But now you have come and I can tell that you are like a daughter to her."

She patted Teresa's cheek before turning back to Lady Swinborne. "Shall we say Tuesday next?"

"You are such a good friend, Sally. Tuesday will be quite convenient."

"I am entirely at your disposal, Lady Jersey. And I must thank you most sincerely for your kind offer. I am greatly looking forward to it," Teresa put in. There, she had said everything right. Now, if there were only some way of making sure she said everything absolutely right next Tuesday, she would be a lot happier.

She and her aunt then bid their hostess a good day. Lady Swinborne insisted on paying two more calls just so she could boast to all she knew of Lady Jersey's personal attention to her niece. Teresa contrived to keep all her comments to platitudes, and thereby managed to not offend anyone.

After returning home, her aunt announced that she was going to lie down for a little nap before the pleasures of the evening.

"I suggest you do the same, Teresa," she said as she mounted the stairs.

"If you do not mind, Aunt Catherine, I would find it much more relaxing if I could go to Lord Merrick's to practice on his pianoforte." Teresa hoped that her aunt would allow this since she was feeling restless from sitting so long. She also was curious as to whether Richard would be there again.

"Oh. Very well. I can see no reason why you should not. Just be sure to return in time to dress for the evening."

"I will. Thank you," Teresa called on her way out the door.

When Teresa entered the music room, she smiled as she noticed the fire in the grate, ready and waiting for her. The room had also been aired, dusted, and swept, losing the musty, unused feel it had had the previous day. It was still just as sparsely furnished, there being only the pianoforte and the two dozen or so gilt chairs arranged in front of it, but as the room was not very large, there was not really a need for much more. A carpet on the hardwood floor might have been nice to mute the slightly hollow sound of the music, but it was not absolutely necessary.

In an effort to forget the tensions of the previous two hours, Teresa played a vigorous piece by her favorite Spanish composer, Antonio Soler. As it required her fingers to fly up and down the keyboard very quickly, Teresa was flushed and out of breath when she finished, but it felt good to release all of her pent-up emotions on the instrument. The applause that followed, however, quite startled her. Her eyes flew to the door, where Richard stood with a half-smile of awe on his handsome face.

Three

Just as on the day before, he was dressed in rather well-worn clothing. His broad shoulders were encased in a coat so tight fitting that Teresa wondered if it wasn't a hand-me-down from the marquis. His breeches, too, seemed almost too tight for his strong, athletic legs, and his boots were the same scuffed old boots he had been wearing the day before. Instead of a proper neckcloth, he had a belcher tie knotted carelessly around his neck. His long dark blond hair was caught back with a black riband despite the current fashion that dictated short hair for gentlemen.

But it was his deep green eyes that really caught Teresa's attention. They looked somehow as if they had seen too much sadness. She wondered if he had ever been a soldier, for he had precisely the same eyes as the weary soldiers who had come to forget their woes in her mother's drawing room.

"I do not believe I have ever seen anyone's fingers move so fast," Richard said, coming farther into the room.

Teresa found herself smiling easily at him. "I believe I play the piece much too fast, but sometimes I need such an outlet."

"An outlet for what?" Richard sat down in the chair

he had occupied the day before when he had been turning pages for her.

Teresa wondered why she was still out of breath. Was it from the last piece she played? Or was it something else? With her newfound awareness of Richard, Teresa felt him to be a little too close for comfort but saw no polite way of saying so. Anyway, perhaps he would need to be close to turn the pages for her again.

Teresa drew a deep breath to calm herself but succeeded only in inhaling the very male scent of him. He smelled clean yet slightly of soot, as if he had been standing too close to a smoking fire.

"An outlet for emotions, tensions, stress," Teresa said seriously but then laughed. "You must think me silly, but I am afraid I find being social quite stressful, and I have just returned from paying morning calls with my aunt."

Richard regarded her rather gravely for a moment. "I had never thought that morning calls could be stressful, but I suppose that they could be if one is unaccustomed to them. You are not used to paying morning calls." It was said more as a statement than a question.

"No. Where I am from, we did not do such things very often."

"Where you are from? You are not English, are you?" Richard looked at her with a rather piercing stare, as if he were trying to figure out just where she was from before she even said it. Yet Teresa was not made uncomfortable by it—rather, it amused her. So far no one in London had asked her where she was from. She supposed they all knew, or else were too polite to ask.

She smiled at him, happy with his directness. "I am half English. That is, my father is English, but my mother is Spanish and I was raised in Spain."

"Ah, that explains the accent. I knew it did not sound French, but I could not place my finger on what it was."

Teresa looked at him, startled for a moment. "I did not realize I had an accent."

Richard smiled. "Yes, you do. A very slight one though, I assure you. Just enough to be intriguing."

When he smiled at her, sitting as close as he was, Teresa felt a warmth rush over her. He had a beautiful smile, showing off his straight white teeth. And, Teresa noted, the smile created a little dimple on his left cheek.

"No one has ever called me intriguing before," Teresa said, cocking her head to one side.

"No? Oh, well, I suppose not. It would be too much for gentlemen of fashion to find anything or anyone intriguing, would it not? Else someone might accuse them of thinking for themselves."

Teresa giggled. "Indeed, sir. They must find everything insipid so as to appear more romantic, I suppose."

Richard's lips twitched with a smile he was clearly trying to hold back. "You have a sharp eye, Miss Seton. However, I believe it is a wise person who has a sharp eye but keeps her equally sharp tongue in its sheath."

"Unfortunately, I have not learned that trick, and it is indeed my sharp tongue that gets me into so much trouble," she said, basking in the unexpected knowledge that he understood her as no one ever had before.

Richard's smile had faded quickly, and once again his face took on its usual serious mien. "It is your quick wit and intelligence, perhaps, that is lost on the idiots of the *ton*. They see only what they want to see, and disparage anyone who behaves any differently than they."

Teresa wished he would smile again but did not quite know how or if she should even try to make him do so again. Suddenly confused by the strange feelings that were running through her, Teresa busied herself with the music in front of her.

She picked the Sonata in C by Haydn from the pile of music she had brought with her and began to play again. Richard turned the pages for her. Although his mouth was not smiling, his brow was clear as he obviously enjoyed the quick tempo.

She continued playing until the clock once again struck five. This time Teresa did not run for the door but instead got up slowly, rather reluctant to end their time together.

Thoughtfully, she moved toward the door, and upon reaching it, she turned around. "Will you be here tomorrow at this same time?"

Richard stood next to the pianoforte. "Yes. I will make sure that I am." He nodded.

And so he was.

A few days later Miss Seton rushed into the music room and immediately began pounding out a march by Mozart. It was not until she was finished that Richard gently put a soothing hand on her shoulder.

Miss Seton jumped. "I did not see you come in, Richard," she said, slightly out of breath.

"Actually, I have been here the whole time. You just did not see me when you ran in," he said, trying unsuccessfully not to smile.

"Oh. I am sorry. How very rude of me." Miss Seton looked at the piano keys in front of her. "I seem to be doing quite a few rude things today," she said with a little hitch in her voice.

"Would you like to tell me about it?" he asked gently.

"It was entirely my fault, I am afraid. I let loose my tongue before thinking through what I was saying. I would not wonder if I am uninvited to a number of parties after this."

"Now, now, I am sure that it cannot have been that bad."

"Oh, but it was!" Miss Seton stood up and paced the room in a very unladylike fashion. "We paid a morning call today at Lady Arundell's, and some gentleman was there I did not know. He was complaining about all the soldiers who have returned from the war, saying that they simply expect to be given jobs when they have no training in doing anything but killing and waging war. He made me so very angry, I simply could not contain myself." Miss Seton's hands had formed themselves into fists as she spoke, and her beautiful expressive eyes flashed with anger and something else as well. Richard could not decide if it was sadness over the mistreatment of the soldiers or embarrassment over her own reaction.

He stood, stepped into her path, and took her fists in his hands. "So you told him he was wrong?"

She looked up at him, turning slightly pink at their intimate contact before turning away and resuming her pacing. "Oh, no, it might have been excusable had I done only that. I am afraid I called him a . . . an unfeeling popinjay who knew nothing about which he spoke. I said that perhaps he should find out for himself just what these soldiers went through for him while he stayed here in the safety of London, engaging in frivolous pursuits."

She turned her worried eyes on him, clearly terribly upset. His laughter died in his throat as a jolt of protectiveness surged through him.

"Oh, Richard," she said rather pathetically, "I said so many rude and terrible things to this gentleman. The entire room hushed at my words."

A giggle escaped from her, catching him off guard, as

she remembered something else. "You should have seen the man's face. It would have been quite amusing had it not been so awful. First he turned white as a ghost and then beet red, and his mouth kept opening and closing like a fish. He had no idea how to respond to me."

Richard shared her amusement, but he was thinking furiously of some way she could extricate herself from this terrible social solecism that she had brought upon herself. "I am afraid the only way out of this would be to apologize to the fellow," Richard said finally, after thinking about it for a minute.

"Oh, no, I could not! Why, then he and everybody else would think that I agreed with him, which I most definitely do not," Miss Seton said with certainty.

"Well, then, the only other alternative is to seek support for your views from like-minded ladies of the *ton*."

This made Miss Seton stop and think. "Yes? But who?"

"Have you ever spoken with Lady Cowper?"

"No. Does she believe the same as I do concerning the plight of these soldiers?" she asked, wide-eyed.

"Yes, I believe that she does. I am not certain, of course," he added hastily, remembering his supposed position, "but it would seem to be a cause that she and her set of politically minded ladies would be interested in. Why don't you ask your aunt? I am sure she would know." Richard paused. "What did your aunt do while you were shooting this fellow down?"

"Nothing, I am afraid. But I could tell that she was extremely embarrassed. In fact, she has not said a word to me at all other than what was strictly necessary since then."

"Hmmm. That is not encouraging, is it?"

"No. I am afraid it is not," Miss Seton said, seating

herself once again at the pianoforte and turning her mind to her music.

While Richard sat and listened, occasionally turning pages for her as necessary, he could not help but admire Miss Seton for her bravery in speaking up in support of the soldiers. He briefly wondered how she knew so much about this issue and why she felt as strongly as she did. Perhaps she had had a brother killed in the war, as he had?

Four

The following Tuesday, with Richard sitting in his usual slightly undersized gilt chair next to her, Teresa was once again playing Beethoven's lovely Fourteenth Sonata.

Toward the end of the piece, she happened to look over at Richard. He was sitting back in his chair with his eyes closed, his hands loosely resting on his lap. A single tear was slowly making its way unheeded down his cheek.

Overcome, she stopped playing and lightly put her hand on his. His eyes flew open and he quickly blinked away the tears that had pooled there.

"Why do you cry?" she asked quietly.

He looked at her with great sadness. "You must forgive me. That sonata is my wife's favorite piece."

"Oh! I did not know you were married." Teresa pulled her hand away, feeling very uneasy. She had unknowingly been meeting a married man.

Richard looked down at his hand and then back up at her. "She . . . she died a year ago. That is the reason for my show of emotion. Please forgive me. I did not mean . . ."

Relief surged through her. "It is no matter. I do not mind you showing your emotions. Not at all. It is the beautiful thing about music, is it not? It bares your emotions in a way that is very difficult to avoid."

She paused for a moment. "How did your wife die?"

Richard drew a shuddering breath. "She was thrown from her horse. She died instantly."

"I am so sorry."

He shook his head. "It is all right. I have just never spoken of it until now."

"Sometimes it is better to speak of such things, difficult though it may be." She wished she herself had the words to comfort him.

Richard smiled wryly. "What would you know of death and other such terrible things?"

Teresa sat up taller. "I know much more than you would think. My mother always hosted the English soldiers who fought in the Peninsular War. Some of them spoke to me of death and the horrors of the battlefield." She looked him directly in the eye. "I have often thought that you looked as if you knew death much more closely than you would admit. I wondered if you were not a soldier yourself."

"No. I have never been a soldier, but I do know death." Richard's eyebrows drew down. "Within the past year, I lost everyone I ever held dear."

Tears stung Teresa's eyes, but she blinked them away quickly. "Oh!" She fought for the right words to say but could find none.

Richard took a deep breath and looked down at his hands, which had clenched in his lap.

Rendered awkward by the silence, Teresa turned back to her music. She quickly selected another piece, deliberately choosing a folk tune that was a little more upbeat.

She played through the piece rather quickly, enjoying the bright melody. However, when she chanced to look

at Richard next to her, he did not seem to be either listening or enjoying the music. He sat lost in his own
thoughts, his brow lowered over his eyes and a slight
frown marring his handsome features.

When she finished, he resumed their conversation as
if he had not been interrupted. "If your mother hosted
so many soldiers in her drawing room, how is it that you
do not enjoy society?" he asked, giving Teresa a glimpse
into the direction his thoughts had taken him.

"I, well, that is, my mother, she—" Teresa stopped,
not knowing quite what to say. Just thinking about her
mother caused her to be as tongue-tied as if they were
actually in the same room. She took a deep breath and
started again. "My mother is very beautiful and witty.
The men who wanted conversation would stay by her."

"What about you? Did you not speak with these soldiers?" Richard said, clearly confused.

"Well, no. I usually sat with those who simply wanted
to talk. They did not expect me to say anything," Teresa
said quietly, looking past Richard toward the window.

"I am sorry, but how could they not expect you to talk
to them?"

"My mother told them not to expect much conversation from me, as I was awkward and had very little to
say anyway." She raised her eyes to his and was surprised to find him looking quite angry. She did not
understand if he was angry with her for being so inept
or with her mother for saying so.

She felt the familiar tight feeling of inadequacy in her
chest but ignored it. She refused to be baited into feeling sorry for herself. "It is true. I really do not have
much conversation. I have come to accept my short-
comings and work around them, like becoming a good
listener and playing the pianoforte."

Richard scowled. Finally, he shifted in his chair so

that he faced her and put his hands on both of her shoulders. Looking directly into her eyes, he said firmly, "Miss Seton, there is nothing wrong with your conversation, nor with you, no matter what your mother may have told you."

Tears stung Teresa's eyes. No gentleman had ever said anything so kind to her. It did not matter whether it was true or not, and she rather believed not. But the gentle yet insistent honesty with which he said it somehow tore at Teresa's heart.

Then, as if to prove his words, he leaned closer, moving his hands from her shoulders to gently cradle either side of her face. Teresa knew he was going to kiss her. She knew she should stop him, but she did not want to.

His lips were firm but soft, gentle but probing, and they made her insides turn to pudding. He tasted slightly salty from the tears he had shed earlier, and she breathed in the clean scent of his shaving soap. His tongue ran along her lips and she parted them for him, reveling in the taste and feel of him. She slid her arms under his coat and around his back. He made her feel so wonderful, so— she tried to form her feelings into words, but her brain would not cooperate, she was so lost in the sensations of his kiss, the feel of his muscular body under her hands. . . .

"Teresa Seton!"

The stern, shocked voice of her aunt rang out in the silent room. Another voice gasped as well.

Teresa and Richard flew apart, and both turned in the direction of the voices.

Lady Swinborne stood just inside the doorway with Lady Jersey at her side. Both looked scandalized at the scene that had been playing out for them.

"Aunt Catherine! What . . . what are you doing here?"

Richard stood up and bowed stiffly to the two ladies.

"What am I doing here? What is *he* doing here? And I thought all this time that you came only to practice the pianoforte." She turned to her friend. "Sally, I assure you, I had no knowledge that my niece was secretly meeting his lordship here."

"No, indeed, how could you? My lord, would you care to explain your presence here, when everyone believes you to be at your estate in the country?" Lady Jersey's lips curled in a smile, while her eyes glittered with nasty glee.

Teresa turned wide eyes upon Richard. "My lord? Richard?"

Lady Swinborne gasped. "Richard, is it? Oh, my, this is much worse than I could possibly have thought!"

Richard stood looking like a deer surrounded by hunters, his eyes darting from one lady to the next. Finally, he said, "It is not at all what you think, Lady Swinborne. We have not been meeting here secretly. That is to say, not intentionally." He then turned to Teresa. "I, ah, perhaps I neglected to mention, Miss Seton . . ."

A laugh burst out from Lady Jersey. "Is it possible, Miss Seton, that you do not know whom you have been kissing?"

Teresa felt her stomach begin to tie itself up into a knot as she, too, stood and faced Richard.

"May I have the honor of making the introduction?" Lady Jersey said with a broad smile. "Miss Seton, it is my pleasure to introduce you to the Marquis of Merrick, known to most as the Merry Marquis."

Teresa automatically sank into a curtsy. Tears stung her eyes as she struggled to hide the anger and hurt she felt. He had lied to her. Why? Why had he not told her that he was the marquis?

Still giggling, Lady Jersey continued. "Now that you

have been properly introduced, I do believe that the marquis might have something to ask of you, Miss Seton?"

Richard looked at Lady Jersey blankly.

Lady Swinborne, however, made everything clear to him when she said, her voice still shuddering with shock, "Indeed, to be caught in so compromising a position."

Teresa was still confused. She watched in surprise as Richard—no, the marquis—turned to her.

With a face that looked as if it were carved out of granite, he said stiffly, "Miss Seton, I would be honored if you would consent to be my wife."

Teresa was shocked. This was entirely her aunt and Lady Jersey's doing. Richard had no desire to be married again just yet. Why, it had been only a year since his wife had died, and he was clearly not over her loss. Not only that, but he did not love her. It was just an accident that they had happened to kiss, and an even worse circumstance that her aunt and Lady Jersey walked in just at that moment.

"No, my lord, I will not consent to be your wife."

With that, she fled from the room.

Five

Richard made a move to go after Miss Seton, but Lady Swinborne put up her hand. "No, my lord, I will go and talk some sense into her. Sally, you will excuse me, I am sure."

Lady Jersey nodded, and then, as her friend left, turned back to Richard, who still stood in shock in the corner of the room. "Well, well, Merry, it has been a much more exciting afternoon than either one of us had expected, has it not?"

Richard dropped into the chair that stood next to him. "You might say that." He paused for a moment before making one more attempt at getting out of this awkward situation. "Lady Jersey, this was completely innocent. Surely you must see that?" He looked up at her intently, as if willing her to forget the whole situation.

"Oh, I am entirely certain that it was unintentional, but whenever is compromising a young lady intentional? No, I am afraid, my lord, that this is too good a story to be kept quiet." Lady Jersey pulled her gloves up higher over her wrists.

Richard scowled but nodded.

"If you will excuse me then, I must spread the word before it is too late to pay any more calls." Lady Jersey swept from the room, giggling with delight at having been present at the conception of the most wonderful piece of gossip.

Richard was shaken. He knew society's rules. Not too long ago he himself had been one its enforcers, delighting, along with everyone else, in the discomfort of those forced to marry after having been caught in a compromising situation. Well, now he was the one who was caught.

He thought back to his time with Miss Seton this past week. He had felt more alive when he was with her than he had for a very long time—since Julia had died. It had felt so good to make her laugh, and to laugh himself. He had nearly forgotten what it was to be happy, but Miss Seton had reminded him. And now he had ruined her.

He stood again, needing to do something, anything, to make her see that she could not reject him. She would be shunned by society! He could not allow that to happen, he thought fiercely. He shook off the thought that she had somehow become indispensable to his own happiness. No, it was for *her* own good that she marry him.

Richard paused for a moment on his way out the door, wryly looking down at his shabby clothing. He quickly turned and headed up the stairs to his bedroom, calling for the housekeeper to bring him some shaving water. If he was going to try to convince Miss Seton to marry him, he needed to be dressed properly.

He had, he thought with a tinge of guilt, deliberately deceived her with his clothes. Oh, not the first time he had met her. Then he had just come in from one of his nearly daily walks through the slums of London, trying to find homeless boys to fill his new orphanage. He knew better than to walk through neighborhoods like St. Giles or Seven Dials dressed in his good clothes. No, it was best that he blend in and look as inconspicuous as possible when out on his forays.

Richard strode to his wardrobe and rifled through his coats, looking for one that was presentable—no, one that was flattering. As he settled on a coat of blue superfine that he had had made for him by Weston two years before, he realized with some amusement that he wanted to look his best for this meeting.

Since he had met Miss Seton, he had made sure he was dressed in his oldest clothes each afternoon when she came to practice—once he had deceived her, there was no easy way to turn back. Moreover, it had felt good that someone liked him for himself and not because he was the Merry Marquis.

And now they were going to be married whether she liked it or not.

Richard nearly nicked himself as he stood shaving. A terrible thought had crossed his mind. He had kissed Miss Seton. Not only that, but it had felt good, sending a familiar warmth through his veins. Julia immediately came to his mind. He had loved her passionately—he still did. So how could he have similar sensations when he kissed Miss Seton? It did not make sense. Richard pushed these disturbing thoughts from his mind and concentrated on not cutting his face.

He dressed as quickly as possible, wishing he still had a valet to help him into his snug coat. He could very well tie his own neckcloth—it just would not be as spectacular as it used to be.

As Teresa ran headlong through her aunt's house, up the stairs, and into her room, she could not contain her tears. She had nearly soaked her pillow when her anger came to the fore.

Tears still streaming down her face, she got up to furiously pace back and forth. How could he? He had lied to her about who he was. What else had he lied to her about? He had been so nice. Was that a lie too? Did he go each night to his club and joke with the other gentlemen about the ugly little girl who said the most outrageous things? She had liked him, trusted him, and believed him when he had said kind things to her. But it was all a lie!

Well, she did not want his friendship or his forced offer of marriage. She stopped her pacing to stare blankly out of the window for a moment. It had been clear that he felt nothing for her except perhaps anger at having been forced to offer for her. And why shouldn't he feel that way? She was no catch—not for an incredibly handsome marquis.

She resumed her pacing. Well, she wanted none of it. None of his pity, his friendship, or his marriage proposal. He could just take it and—

Her thought was interrupted by a knock at her bedroom door.

"Teresa, may I come in?" her aunt called from the other side. Without waiting for an answer, Lady Swinborne entered the room.

"Well, what have you to say for yourself, Teresa? I hope you are satisfied with your day's work." Lady Swinborne frowned down at her niece.

Teresa knew that her aunt was furious with her, but she was slightly comforted by the touch of sympathy she detected in her aunt's voice. "You have every right to be angry with me."

"I most certainly do. I have been working hard these past weeks trying to push you forward. I have introduced you to most of the eligible men of the *ton,* and you have done nothing but make things difficult. Hiding behind plants, making inappropriate comments at times, and saying nothing at all the rest of the time. I have been at my wit's end. And then I had to put up with all of this homeless-soldier nonsense. Honestly, Teresa!"

Teresa stood quietly, accepting her aunt's scolding, knowing full well that it was deserved.

Lady Swinborne settled herself in the chair directly in front of the fire. "I had little hope for making a brilliant match for you, I admit. But I had thought that at least a respectable one was possible. But now . . . now you have completely ruined yourself."

"He lied to me, Aunt Catherine," Teresa said, angrily wiping the tears from her face.

This was too much for Lady Swinborne. Her voice rose again despite her attempt to control it. "You kissed him!"

"He lied. He told me he took care of the house."

"I can assure you it would not have been any better had he been the caretaker of the house." Lady Swinborne paused for a moment to regain control over her emotions. She then continued in what she evidently thought was a reasonable tone. "It is your extreme good fortune that he turned out to be the marquis and not the steward. No, you could not have done any better for yourself than to marry the Marquis of Merrick. You may consider yourself very lucky."

"But he does not *want* to marry me," Teresa said. By the expression on her aunt's face, she could immediately see that this statement did nothing to help her case. She tried another tack. "Aunt Catherine, I do not love him, and he does not love me."

"Love! What does love have to say to any of this?" Lady Swinborne exploded again.

"I promised Papa I would not marry without love," Teresa said quietly, remembering the conversation she had had with her father just before leaving. He had been in his bed, too weak to get up after his heart had failed him for the second time within three months. He had held her hand and implored her to do as he had done, and marry someone who truly made her happy. Someone she loved and who loved and cherished her in return.

"Well, a bigger fool there never was than your papa," Lady Swinborne exclaimed. "Did he make you promise such nonsense?"

Teresa nodded, and held back a new wave of tears as thoughts of her beloved papa flooded through her mind.

Lady Swinborne frowned. "Well, let me tell you, Teresa, that most people of our class do not marry for love. Do you think that I loved Swinborne when I married him? I did not. But I grew to love him. The past five years since he died have been a very difficult time for me. We had grown very close." Lady Swinborne blinked rapidly before turning her back to her niece. "Your father was a besotted fool when he married your mother and settled permanently in Madrid, and I am sure that it brought him nothing but heartache.

"But I shall say no more on that head." She pursed her lips together, as if she were literally swallowing her words. "Meanwhile, I am sure that in the past half hour Lady Jersey has been busy telling everyone and anyone about this fiasco."

Teresa's eyes went wide at this thought. She truly was ruined.

Seeing her stricken expression, her aunt softened her stern face for a moment before turning grave once more. "I am glad this has finally gotten through to you. I am sorry for it, my dear, but you no longer have a choice. You will marry Lord Merrick, and you will thank him most kindly for doing what is right."

Teresa flinched at the harsh reality in her aunt's words and turned to look longingly out of the window.

"I am sure that Lord Merrick will come this evening to formalize the arrangements. Until he does, I suggest that you think about what has occurred and be grateful that Merrick is a man of honor."

Teresa did not reply but rested her head against the window frame. She heard an exasperated sigh, and then the click of the door. Aunt Catherine left her to her own thoughts.

She wondered briefly what her aunt had meant about her father being filled with heartache. She knew that he loved her mother beyond anything, though she was rather unsure whether this love was reciprocated. In her drawing room, Doña Isabella had been equally generous with her attention and favors to all the men around her. Surely, she loved her husband the most and just did not show it in public?

Now was not the time to think about her parents. She had more pressing concerns, like her own ruined reputation. She was faced with the awful alternatives of either being married to a man who did not love her or being scorned by society and never married at all.

Yet, somehow, when she tried to think about it now, she felt nothing. Nothing but an overwhelming sadness at the unfairness of life.

Six

Richard took one last look in the mirror, adjusted his neckcloth, and then shrugged. It would have to do. He did not have a valet, and his clothes were at least a year out of fashion anyway.

He was just about to leave his room, when a knock sounded on the door. He opened it to reveal his Scottish housekeeper.

"Ah, Mrs. MacPherson, I am glad you are here. I am going out this evening."

"Aye, m'lord?"

"I, ah, I am going to propose to Miss Seton," he continued, a little embarrassed.

"My felicitations."

Richard wasn't sure, but he thought he heard relief in her voice. His lips twitched with a smile, but he restrained himself. "Yes, thank you."

"M'lord, I hope ye dinna mind my plain speakin', but if ye would be marrying agin, would ye nae be wantin' to hire a staff once more?"

Richard immediately recognized the wisdom in this. "Yes, indeed. You are absolutely correct. I shall send tomorrow for Samuel, my butler, to return to us from Merrick Hall and tell him to bring any staff he feels necessary."

Mrs. MacPherson nodded. "Thank ye, m'lord." She

turned to go but then turned back. "I am sorry, m'lord, the reason I coom up was that this was just delivered. A wee lad is awaitin' below stairs for a reply."

It was a hastily scrawled note from Mrs. Long, the headmistress of his orphanage. He quickly skimmed over the contents, letting loose a series of expletives that would have burned the ears of any proper lady. Fortunately, his housekeeper did not have such fine sensibilities.

He remembered himself, and apologized to her anyway, adding, "Tell the boy to run back and I will follow as quickly as I can."

What had happened to all the staff he had hired to take care of the boys? He had gone to no small expense to find a suitable building to house them and then had hired no less than six footmen and maids to care for them. He had interviewed dozens of women to act as headmistress and had finally hired the one he felt would be both firm yet loving. Was the woman so totally ineffectual that she could not control twenty boys with the help of the rest of the staff?

Richard's annoyance simmered in the pit of his stomach as he tried to find a hackney as quickly as possible.

Richard could hear the screams from the street even before he entered the orphanage. Gritting his teeth, he strode directly to the dining room, from where much of the noise seemed to be emanating.

He stood in the doorway, his mouth hanging open for a moment. It was complete mayhem. Mrs. Long stood near the door, wringing her hands, while nearly all of the boys were engaged in fighting one another. A few stood on the sidelines cheering their comrades on. Chairs lay every which way, some broken into pieces. The large dining table was pushed askew, and two boys were on top of it pummeling each other. The screams, cries, and shouts of the boys filled the air.

"Stop!" Richard bellowed at the top of his voice.

He was ignored by many, but some of the boys did stop whatever it was they were doing and look toward him. He strode over to the table where the two boys were still fighting, but undermined his commanding entrance by slipping on something slick on the floor. He quickly regained his balance and, avoiding the flailing fists of the upper child, picked him up and removed him from the table. No sooner had he put the child down than the boy moved to return to his fight.

Richard tried to stop him but instead received a swift kick to his shin and a slew of words that made his own ears burn. As he grabbed at his injured leg, the boy raced around him, climbed back onto the table, and resumed the pummeling of his opponent.

The rest of the boys, seeing how ineffectual Richard was at stopping this fight, went on with their own, and soon the room was as it had been when he first entered it.

Swallowing both his exasperation and his pride, Richard tried again. He separated boys, yelled for quiet, and got hit and punched quite a few times. He slipped and fell on his indignity at least twice. One boy turned his frustration on him, pulling at his neckcloth, his hair, and landing a rather good blow to his gut before he was able to finally capture the child's hands and bring an end to the assault.

By the time Richard had finally put a stop to most of the fighting, his naturally merry disposition had dissolved the ill feelings he had harbored when he first walked onto the scene.

He looked around at the now-quiet room. Broken crockery littered the floor, and it was obvious that there had been a food fight before the boys had let loose on one another. Splotches of mashed potatoes decorated both the walls and not a few of the boys. An overturned pudding dripped from the table onto the floor. Limp spinach leaves hung from a wall sconce—the bowl that once held the vegetable was in pieces on the floor underneath. And a chicken carcass, picked clean of all its meat, was skewered onto the center candle of the candelabra in the middle of the table.

The sight of the bedraggled boys and the food-strewn room made Richard lose the last of his self-control. Unable to contain himself, he burst out laughing. His heart and his head felt light, as if he hadn't a care in the world. He was filthy and exhausted, but it felt so good to laugh.

The boys all looked at one another in a confused way. Then, almost in unison, they looked back at Richard as if he had completely lost his mind. Mrs. Long, too, looked as if she wondered if he had been hit on the head so hard that he had lost his senses. Richard's laughter, however, was infectious, and a few of the boys stopped crying and began to giggle with him.

He finally regained control of himself and managed to wipe the smile from his face, but the laughter was still in his eyes when he finally spoke. "Mrs. Long, would you be so good as to tell me what started all this?"

The woman came forward a step, unsure of how close she wanted to get to someone who was clearly mentally unbalanced. "Well, milord, I don't rightly know fer sure. Alls I know is that they was sitting and finishing their dinner when suddenly this fight broke out. All the boys started fightin' and throwin' food, and that's when I sent round the note for you to come."

Richard nodded. "Thank you, Mrs. Long. And the footmen and maids who were supposed to be here?"

"They left as soon as the food started flyin', milord."

"I see." He then schooled his face and voice to be as serious as he could muster, pulled down his eyebrows, and turned to the boys. "Would someone care to tell me what started this fight?"

All the boys began talking at once.

"He took more than his share of dessert," from one boy.

"No, I didn't," came back from the one accused.

"Jack-o said he didn't want no dessert," from another.

"Did not," from a fourth.

The arguing began once more, but when they raised their fists at one another, Richard intervened before all hell broke loose again.

"All right!" he shouted. "I get the point. There will be no dessert served for the next two weeks. You will all clean up this room until it shines. Tomorrow you will fix any chairs that have been broken. And if I ever hear of anything like this happening again, you will get more severe punishments. Is that clear?"

There was quiet in the room, except from the maligned Jack-o, who stood crying near the potato-splattered wall. Richard moved over and knelt in front of the child. Pulling him gently onto his lap, he spoke softly to him. "It's all right, Jack-o. Don't cry."

"It's all my fault," the boy hiccoughed.

"No, no. It is all right. You did not start the fight. This probably would have happened no matter what."

Richard pressed the boy's damp head to his shoulder, pointedly not thinking about what part of the meal could possibly be in his hair to make it wet.

Little arms wrapped themselves around his neck and gave a squeeze. Gently, he squeezed back before pulling away a little to give the boy a smile. The child had stopped crying, and used the back of Richard's sleeve to wipe his runny nose.

Smothering back the impulse to snatch his arm away from the urchin, Richard stood up and looked about the

room once more. "Mrs. Long, you will please take one
or two boys with you and bring up any cleaning supplies
needed. The rest of you will begin by picking up all of
the chairs and putting them off to the side. Take the broken chairs and place them in the hallway."

It took them only a little over an hour to completely
clean the room, remove all the broken dishes, and clear
off the remainder of the meal from the walls, floor, and
table. Once everything was back to rights, Richard
looked around the room at twenty exhausted boys. A
few sprawled in the remaining chairs, while some
leaned against the wall, too tired to hold themselves up
anymore.

Richard smiled at them and gently cuffed one boy
across his head. The boy grinned up at him. "Yer looking
rather dapper this evening', guv. Goin' out someplace?"

Richard looked down at his clothes. His favorite blue
coat and breeches were covered with food, his waistcoat
had lost two buttons, his neckcloth was untied, his shirt-
front had gotten orange spots all over it, and he really
did not want to think about what was on his sleeve. To
add insult to injury, he had somehow lost the ribbon that
had held his hair back, and his boots were scratched. It
was only then that he remembered exactly where he was
supposed to have been.

"Damnation! I completely forgot about Teresa!"
Richard dropped his head into his hands.

"Teresa? 'Oos that, guv? Yer gal?"

Richard scowled more at himself than at the boys.
"She is going to be my wife, and I was supposed to have
been proposing to her this evening." He pulled out his
pocket watch and checked the time. It was much too late
to call upon her now.

A couple of the boys looked sympathetically at

Richard. "She'll fergive ya, gov, don't worry. Jus' bring 'er some flowers or sweets. Gals like that kinda thing."

"A gee-gaw'll do the trick, milord, you take my word on it," one of the older boys suggested.

Richard smiled and nodded. "Yes. I think that is just what I will do. Now, off to bed with all of you."

There was some grumbling at this, but the boys all went trooping upstairs to their respective rooms.

Mrs. Long reappeared a few minutes later after putting away the last of the cleaning things. She looked distinctly nervous and had gone back to wringing her hands. "Oh, milord, I don't know what we would've done if you 'adn't come," she said tragically.

"It's all right, Mrs. Long. Tomorrow you can see about hiring a new staff. One that will not desert you when you need them most."

"Yes, milord! Oh, thank you, milord." Mrs. Long curtsied gratefully.

After a moment's thought, Richard asked, "What sort of exercise do the boys receive during the day?"

"Exercise, milord? Why, I don't believe that they git any."

Richard shook his head. "That, then, is the problem. I believe it is lack of exercise that started this whole thing, Mrs. Long. You should allow them some free time to run and play in the park every day. I will purchase some balls and a cricket bat and have them delivered here. Boys need plenty of running around—something we completely forgot when making up their daily schedule."

Mrs. Long beamed up at Richard, relief evident in her eyes. "Yes, milord. Plenty of exercise every day is what they'll git."

Richard said good night and left to find a hackney to take him home. Goodness, he was tired! But it was a good sort of tired. In fact, he wasn't sure why, but he felt quite fulfilled by his evening's activities. Perhaps it was just what he needed too, a little exercise and playing with the boys. As he collapsed into his bed after stripping off his ruined clothing, he decided to be sure to join the boys at least once a week during their playtime in the park.

Seven

"It was not well done of you, my lord. What was poor Teresa to think when you did not come yesterday evening?"

Teresa froze, her hand lightly resting on the doorknob. Her aunt's stern voice carried clearly through the partly open door.

"I will repeat my apologies to Miss Seton, Lady Swinborne, but as I told you, it could not be helped." Richard sounded tired, as if this were not the first or perhaps even the second time he had apologized.

"I should think that a proposal of marriage would take precedence over anything."

"Lady Swinborne, I have told you, it was an important matter that required my immediate attention." The tone of his voice told Teresa that he was beginning to lose his patience.

The floorboard under Teresa creaked as she shifted her weight. They would have heard her. Now she had no choice but to go into this embarrassing situation.

Taking a deep breath, Teresa entered the room and closed the door firmly behind her so as to give the footman standing in the hallway as little as possible to report to the others below stairs.

"Ah, Teresa. Here is Lord Merrick, finally," her aunt said with a pointed look at Richard.

Teresa looked at him and felt her heart stop. This was not the same man she had kissed yesterday. This was not the Richard with whom she had become friends. Here was a lord of the realm, resplendent in his exquisitely tailored bottle-green coat, tight-fitting breeches, tastefully embroidered waistcoat, and well-tied cravat. This was the Marquis of Merrick.

She felt herself color as she remembered his kiss and the feel of his hard muscles against her. When she had run her hands under his coat as he had kissed her, she had been able to feel the heat of his body through the thin backing of his waistcoat, almost as if the cloth had not been there. Her fingers tingled as she remembered the sensation.

But now he stood there, looking like an Adonis, complete with long, shining blond hair and broad shoulders. His clothes were a bit out-of-date, but that did not diminish his commanding presence. That this gentleman was here to see her, to propose marriage to her, was beyond belief. She fought a strong urge to run and hide.

"I brought some flowers for you, Miss Seton. I hope you like them." Richard bowed and offered her a beautiful bouquet of tulips.

She accepted the flowers with a little curtsy but was unable to force an appropriate word from her suddenly constricted throat. She sat down close to her aunt on the white brocade settee.

Lady Swinborne, however, was not inclined to serve as a shield. She rose immediately, saying, "I am sure you two have much to discuss. I shall see that these flowers are put into a proper vase and return in precisely half an hour." She gave her niece a pointed look and added, "I expect everything to be settled by then."

Teresa watched her aunt leave the room and felt suddenly bereft of all support. She could not do this. She could not sit and talk with this gentleman all alone. She felt herself begin to panic and looked wildly about the room for some way to escape. There was no pianoforte to hide behind. There was no one but herself and the Marquis.

Her gaze slipped over Richard and then flew back to him. He was looking at her with such concern in his eyes. Could he sense her fear? He leaned toward her from his chair across the carpet.

It must have been the expression in his sad eyes. Her fear began to evaporate, and, in its place, her anger from the day before returned with full force. She looked at him, this fine gentleman, and remembered how easily he had lied to her, and how he had hurt her with his false kindness.

Richard's voice finally broke through the stillness that had settled on them. "Miss Seton . . . Teresa . . ." He stopped.

Teresa tilted her head. "My lord?"

"Richard."

"What is it that you were going to say, my lord?" Teresa said, ignoring his correction.

Richard frowned, but then smoothed his features into an expression of sincere contrition. "Teresa, I apologize."

"Apologize for what? For lying to me or for kissing me?" she queried, a hard edge to her voice.

"I did not exactly lie to you."

"Oh, no? What do you call it, then? Perhaps my English is not as good as I had thought. You told me you took care of the house."

"I do take care of the house," Richard defended himself weakly.

"Yes. It belongs to you. You must have simply forgotten to mention that little detail." Teresa could not stop the sarcasm.

Richard glared at her, his hands clenched. "I, I did not intend to lie. But I did not want you to tell everyone that you had met the Marquis of Merrick at his home. I have not let anyone know that I am in town. Also, you would not have been able to come and practice on my pianoforte if your aunt had known that I was there."

If he imagined that she was going to forgive him on that flimsy excuse, Teresa thought to herself, he was sadly mistaken. She was still very angry, and she was not going to make this easy for him. She looked at him, carefully keeping her expression impassive.

Richard stood up and faced her. "Teresa, the point is that now you *have* to marry me. I am sorry if that is not what you had wanted or expected, but that is just the way it needs to be."

"Why does it need to be that way? It was only my aunt and Lady Jersey who saw us, and it was only one little kiss." Teresa realized that she was now the one making weak excuses.

"You know that Lady Jersey is one of the biggest gossips in London. She herself said yesterday that she was going out immediately to spread the word of your downfall."

Teresa opened her mouth to refute this but found that in all honesty she could not—her aunt had told her as much the day before. She was ruined, and there was nothing she could do about it. She thought longingly for home and the comfort of her father's side.

"I promised Papa I would marry for love," she said quietly, a tear escaping from the corner of her eye. She brushed it away quickly, but clearly not fast enough.

In a moment he was on his knees in front of her. "Teresa, I am so sorry."

Teresa noticed that he no longer smelled of soot. No, now he had a very male smell of soap and spicy bay rum shaving lotion. She resisted the temptation to lean closer so she could smell him better.

He grasped her hands strongly in his own, bringing her mind back to the problem at hand. "Teresa, you must marry me to save your reputation, but I promise you, it will simply be a marriage of convenience."

His hands were firm and warm on her own, but his words were like ice to her heated dreams of love. She tried to remove her hands from his grip, but his fingers only tightened around hers.

"My lord, I will not agree to such a scheme. I cannot," she said with as much conviction as she could.

His grip tightened, as if he could bend her to his will simply by force. Teresa winced at the pressure but forced herself to remain silent.

Finally, he let go of her and stood. Running his hands through his hair, he looked down at her and shook his head in exasperation. "Perhaps you do not understand, Teresa. No one will marry you. You will not be able to marry for love, for there will be no one with whom you could fall in love. Your invitations will stop altogether. Even your aunt will be shunned by society."

Teresa felt a constriction in her throat. Her aunt would suffer? They would be shunned? No, he had to be lying again. How could she possibly trust him? This man who had said that she was beautiful, who had lied to her about his identity, who had kissed her with such tenderness and then left her to attend to some other business while she waited in vain for him to come and do the right thing by her. It was true that he had come, but not for nearly twenty-four hours. No, he was clearly untrustworthy.

Teresa raised her chin a fraction of an inch and spoke her mind. "I do not believe you. I do not trust you."

Richard's eyebrows drew down over his eyes, and she knew he was extremely angry and hurt by her words.

"You still do not believe me? You wound me, Teresa, but at this point you have no choice but to trust me. You will marry me." His voice was firm.

"No."

Teresa would not back down. She looked him directly in the eye.

He was the first to blink. "You are a stubborn woman, Teresa Seton. I am proposing a marriage of convenience to save your damned reputation. I did not say that we needed to stay married forever. You can still go to parties and look for your true love. And when you find him, we will have our marriage annulled. You will be free to marry again and you will be untouched by me, so you can assure the gentleman that any children you have will be his. What more do you want?" His words were clipped and short.

There was no doubt that he was angry, but there was also no doubt that what he was offering was the best thing Teresa could ever hope for in this situation.

She looked up at him looming over her, considering his proposal carefully. "The marriage can be annulled?"

"Yes, quite easily. I need only fill out the marriage license incorrectly. You can protest the error and our marriage will be declared null and void."

Teresa's already large eyes widened. "You would do all this for me?"

The tension in the room lessened considerably. "Yes. I like you, Teresa, and I do not want to ruin your life due to my indiscretion."

She nodded, finally coming to a decision. It was not one that she liked, but if it would save her aunt from social censure, she would have to live with it. "Thank you, Richard. You are very kind to me."

He smiled and relaxed. "Not at all. If I were truly kind to you, I would never have gotten you into this mess at all."

Teresa tilted her head. "You are sorry, then, to have kissed me?"

His lips twitched for a moment at her unintentional flirting, but then his face became serious. "No. I am afraid that I am not at all sorry for that."

Teresa felt her color rise hotly to her face at his provocative words, and the huskiness of his voice as he said it. All of a sudden, the room felt too small to contain the both of them.

The door opened just then, and her aunt came loudly into the room. Teresa was never so happy to see her aunt as she was at that moment.

Richard turned toward her. "Everything is settled, Lady Swinborne." Then, putting his hand into his pocket, he pulled out a small box. "I almost forgot. This is for you." He handed the box to Teresa.

A brilliant ruby surrounded by diamonds sparkled up at her. She gasped as she took out the magnificent ring.

Richard took it from her hand and slipped it onto her finger.

"It was my mother's engagement ring, and my grandmother's before her. There is, in fact, a whole matching set, but I think I will give that to you after we are married," Richard said with a twinkle in his eye.

Teresa could barely keep her eyes from the beautiful ring on her finger. No one had ever given her anything so lovely.

Lady Swinborne nodded approvingly. "I believe we should begin planning a ball to be held in honor of your marriage. To ensure that the gossips have as little to discuss as possible. We must be certain to show that this alliance has the full approval of both families. Have you discussed when the wedding will be?"

Richard sat down again, clearly realizing that this interview was far from over. "No, we had not. When do you think would be appropriate?"

Lady Swinborne sat down as well, and thought about this for a moment. "I do not think we should wait for the banns to be posted. One week, perhaps two? It is a lot to be done in that short a time, but we cannot risk taking too much longer, since it will be public knowledge by this evening exactly why you are getting married."

Richard nodded. "I will get a special license. That is not a problem. A ball is probably a good idea, although I do not have much family left to approve or not."

"Surely you have aunts and uncles. I know that you have your cousin, Mr. Fotheringay-Phipps."

Richard's lips twitched with laughter. "Ah, yes. Poor Fungy, he will be so put out when he hears that I am to be married again. He is next in line for my title," he explained to Teresa.

Teresa felt quite excluded from this conversation. In all honesty, it really did not matter when they were married, since it would not change the fact that it would be a loveless marriage.

What was worrying her most at the moment was the ball. How would she manage being the center of attention at a ball held in her honor? It scared the wits out of her just thinking about it. "Are you sure that we need to hold a ball, Aunt Catherine?" she said, finally voicing her fears.

Lady Swinborne looked up from her thoughts to scrutinize her niece. "Yes, my dear, I am certain of it. I will even write to invite your Uncle Abington, although I am not at all certain that he would come, as he very rarely comes to town. But it would be a boon were he and Erwina to attend. And you, young lady," Lady Swinborne wagged a finger in Teresa's direction, "will not shirk your duties and hide behind the foliage as you are wont to do."

Teresa felt the heat rise in her cheeks once again as she stole a look at Richard. He was looking rather serious, and not a little worried. Perhaps with Richard at her side, she thought, she would be able to untie her tongue.

Lady Swinborne continued. "I believe it would be best if you, my lord, were to be seen escorting Teresa from now on."

Richard gulped audibly but quickly coughed to try to cover it up. "You truly feel that to be necessary? Perhaps I can begin after the wedding . . ."

"You will begin this very evening," Lady Swinborne said in her most stern voice. "We will be attending Lady Anson's soiree."

Teresa looked sympathetically at Richard. An idea came to mind, and she acted on it immediately. "Oh, no, Aunt Catherine. He surely could not do so tonight. Why, just look at his clothes! They are sadly out of fashion. I am sure that Lord Merrick has not been to his tailor in nearly a year."

Richard jumped at Teresa's opening. "Indeed, I have not! It would be most inappropriate of me to attend any social gathering dressed in my outmoded clothing, Lady Swinborne. And Teresa should certainly not be seen in public without me. I am afraid that you are going to have to either cancel your plans for the next week or simply go alone."

He turned away from Lady Swinborne and gave Teresa a wink and a smile. Teresa could not contain her giggle, but put her hand to her mouth to stifle it as best as she could.

Lady Swinborne looked from one to the other, a frown on her face. Then her stern visage eased a bit around the corners. "I think this match is better made than any of us had previously thought."

Eight

Lady Swinborne had finally allowed that Richard could not attend any social functions until he had seen to his wardrobe, but she did not dismiss her niece. Unfortunately, her insistence on Teresa attending the soiree that evening was quickly found to be a mistake after all.

Lady Anson had been all that was good and kind when they first arrived. "My dear Miss Seton, am I to understand that congratulations are in order?" she had gushed without reserve.

Teresa felt her cheeks warm as Lady Swinborne responded in like manner. "Oh, to be sure, my dear Lady Anson!" she had said enthusiastically. "Indeed, we are extremely lucky that Teresa has done so well as to catch the eye of one so eminently suitable."

After this warm welcome, though, Lady Swinborne's friends did not swarm toward her as readily as usual. Teresa was relieved not to be immediately surrounded and forced to make her attempts at polite conversation. But soon she grew uncomfortable in the realization that instead of people coming up to speak to them directly, there were whispers and guarded glances shot in their direction. Looking at her aunt, she found that Lady Swinborne's smile had also become forced.

Teresa was relieved when she noticed the young lady she had met at Lady Jersey's standing nearby. Miss Peyton saw Teresa at the same time, and had turned to speak to her, when her mother caught her arm.

"Prudence, you are not to speak to that girl. Caught in such a compromising position. You do not want to be seen associating with such people, my dear. You have your own reputation to think about." Lady Peyton's whisper was loud enough to be heard by those around her.

Teresa opened her mouth to comment on the unfairness of such cavalier treatment—as if it were her fault she had been kissed and caught. Her aunt, however, spoke first, taking her arm and pointedly turning her back to the rude woman. "My dear Teresa, just look about you. Why, there is not a girl here who will do as well as you have done. To have the esteem and affection of such a handsome and wealthy marquis is something that no other young lady will be able to boast of this season."

A rather loud "harrumph" was heard as Lady Peyton and her daughter moved away, followed by a few appreciative titters from the ladies standing just behind Teresa and her aunt.

Teresa looked at her aunt with gratitude and said quietly, "You are very kind, Aunt Catherine."

"What? I speak only the truth, my dear," Lady Swinborne said, patting her niece's arm affectionately.

Just before they were about to turn toward the refreshment table, they were approached by a trio of gentlemen. Two were dressed with elegant distinction. The third, however, was attired to such a degree of ridiculousness that Teresa had a hard time keeping her laughter from escaping.

So high were his shirt points, and so bright the many gold buttons on his green-and-gold-embroidered waistcoat and sharply cut away lemon-yellow tailcoat that Teresa almost felt as if she needed to shield her eyes from his magnificence. He sported no less than five fobs, and his matching yellow breeches were so tight that she was sure he would not be able to sit were he given the opportunity.

His clothes were evidently cut to show off his fine figure. Teresa, however, could not help but remember that Richard's shoulders were somewhat broader and his legs much more muscular than this fine gentleman's, even though the two were probably about the same height.

The Exquisite bowed with a flourish over her aunt's hand.

"My dear Lady Swinborne, such a pleasure to see you here this evening," he drawled.

Lady Swinborne's face had become wreathed in smiles at the gentleman's approach. Now she almost giggled like a young girl at his exaggerated attention. "The pleasure is entirely mine, dear sir."

He bowed his head graciously and then said, "Would you do the honors?"

Lady Swinborne looked perplexed for a moment, and then, with a guilty look, remembered her niece's presence. "Oh, of course. Miss Teresa Seton, may I present Lord Merrick's cousin, the Honorable St. John Fotheringay-Phipps?"

Teresa curtsied as the gentleman kissed the air just over the back of her gloved hand.

"I am given to understand, Miss Seton, that you are soon to become one of the family?" Mr. Fotheringay-Phipps drawled. He somehow managed to maintain his facade of boredom while scrutinizing her rather closely.

"I, er, yes, that is correct. Your cousin was kind enough to offer for my hand today," Teresa stammered, overcome by the gentleman's inspection.

He finally nodded with apparent approval. "Well, in

that case, please call me Fungy. Might even venture to call me cousin."

"Thank you, ah, Cousin Fungy."

"I say, Fungy, would you mind?" one of his companions complained.

Teresa redirected her gaze to the two gentlemen standing just behind him. While both maintained the quiet elegance prescribed by Beau Brummell, one of them was quite remarkable in his dark coloring. Teresa realized that he must be the Eurasian peer who had taken society by storm a few years earlier. While he seemed good-humored and easygoing, his companion was more saturnine, with slashing eyebrows dominating a devilishly handsome face.

"Ah, truly sorry. Lady Swinborne, Miss Seton, may I present Julian Ritchie, the Earl of Huntley, and Sinclair Stratton, Viscount Reath?" Fungy said, pointing first to the darker gentleman and then to the other.

While the gentlemen bowed to the two ladies, Fungy turned back to Teresa and asked, "So, where is Merry?"

"Merry?" Teresa asked, perplexed.

"Lord Merrick," said Lord Reath.

"M'cousin," Fungy replied at the same time.

"Yes, you remember him. Tall man, rather fair, blond hair. You are engaged to marry him?" Lord Huntley added with a smile twinkling in his turquoise eyes.

Fungy turned to him. "Well, everyone is fair to you, my noble nabob."

Teresa's eyes widened, but Lord Huntley just laughed at the teasing remark.

"Yes, so, where is he?" Lord Reath said again, redirecting everyone to the problem at hand.

"Richard was unable to join us this evening," Teresa said quickly.

"Richard?" Lord Huntley asked.

"Who is Richard?" Lord Reath asked simultaneously as if completing Huntley's thought.

"Richard? Why, that is Merry's Christian name, isn't it? Haven't heard anyone call him that since . . . well, egads, don't think I've ever heard anyone call him that," said Fungy, rather perplexed.

"That . . . that is what he asked me to call him," Teresa said, smiling at Fungy's bewilderment.

"Did he?" the three said in unison.

Teresa covered her mouth to hide her giggle. She was glad to see that even Lady Swinborne's lips twitched at the antics of the three gentlemen.

Teresa became serious once again, and said, "Rich . . . ah, Lord Merrick, had a small problem and was not able to come."

"What sort of problem?" asked Fungy.

"What sort of problem could a man, who has been living in seclusion for a year, have?" Lord Reath asked, raising one devilish eyebrow.

"Yes, one who has not even seen his very closest friends for that time, I might add," Lord Huntley agreed.

The three turned to look at her rather accusingly.

Teresa turned pink with their scrutiny. Now that she was the focus of the combined attention of all three, she felt overwhelmed and a little panicked. "It . . . it is precisely because he has not been out in so long that he had this, ah, problem." Teresa was having a hard time trying not to stammer and to order her words coherently.

She took a deep breath to try to control her rapidly beating heart. These men, she told herself, were Richard's friends and meant well. "You see, it is his lack of proper clothing. He needs to see his tailor." She looked imploringly at Fungy. "I am sure you understand, Cousin?"

"Humph!" Lord Huntley and Lord Reath said together.

"Oh! Indeed, yes. Very important." Fungy, at least, showed some sympathy. The other two were clearly unimpressed.

The three men bowed to the two ladies, took their leave, and went off to discuss this turn of events in private.

"Well, of all the chicken-hearted . . ." she heard Reath drawl as they moved away from her and her aunt.

Teresa looked at her aunt, feeling slightly dazed, as if she had just been an unwitting partner in a farce. Her aunt looked very much the same way, and could only give her niece a weak smile.

The evening went rapidly downhill. For the next two hours they endured set-downs, nasty looks, and downright rude curiosity from those they had called friends and acquaintances. Even Lady Swinborne could not stand any more after some time, and called for their carriage, ending their evening at a much earlier hour than usual.

Richard stepped into the back hallway of his house and was amazed at the difference a few maids could make to a house. No longer was there a solitary candle burning to greet him, but a lamp, which brightened the entrance considerably. The table was dusted, the floor swept clean, and the fresh smell of recently polished wood filled the air. Richard was also rather surprised to see his housekeeper advancing on him in a very determined way.

"M'lord, there are three men here who dinna want to leave 'til they've had a word with ye," she said. The straight line of her mouth bespoke her disapproval. "I told them that ye were out, but they scoffed and said they would wait 'til ye returned."

Richard drew his eyebrows down, trying to think of who might be calling on him. Then he noticed the small tray in the housekeeper's hand, and took up the three cards there. Unable to repress the smile that split his face, he started up the back stairs to his room.

"Tell them I'll be with them shortly," he called out as he took the stairs two at a time.

He changed into his buff-colored riding breeches. The leather was in poor condition, but it was the best he could do. At least his coat of pale yellow superfine was still in fashion, although the buttons were rather large and showy compared to the more understated ones currently worn by the dandies. A quick, simple knot in his neckcloth finished his toilette.

He paused for a moment to take a deep breath before entering the drawing room a mere fifteen minutes later. He had not seen his closest friends for nearly a year, when he had taken his knocker off the door and left town to bury his beloved Julia.

Julia was the fourth and last person to be buried in his family plot at Merrick. The three others, his mother, sister, and brother, had come in quick succession just months before. He had returned to town a mere two weeks later, unable to bear the silence of his ancestral home, but had preferred for the world to think him still in the country, mourning his family. The knocker had stayed off the door, and he had contacted no one since then. But now he knew he had no choice but to reenter the world from which he had turned away. With his proposal to Teresa he had committed himself to this. Now was the time to start.

His friends looked very comfortable lounging negligently around his drawing room as they waited for him.

They had made themselves comfortable, as they had always done before. Richard noticed, with a wry smile, that they had helped themselves to his finest brandy.

Huntley pushed himself away from the intricately carved marble mantelpiece against which he had been leaning. "Well, Merry, it's about time you showed up."

"Kept us waiting long enough!" Reath complained from his seat on the maroon-and-white-striped sofa.

"Damn, but Cousin Teresa was right about your clothes!" Fungy said, coming over from the window, where he had been staring out at the passersby in the square.

"It is good to see you too," Richard said, shaking each of his friends' hand. "Cousin Teresa?" he added, giving Fungy a rather piercing stare.

Completely ignoring the look, Fungy easily replied, "Yes, Cousin Teresa. That is what I should be calling your intended, is it not, er . . . Richard?"

Reath barked out a laugh, while Huntley immediately fell into a coughing fit.

Richard gave the two men his fiercest glare. "Would you gentlemen care to share the joke? And why are you calling me by my given name? Never have before."

"It is what Miss Seton called you," Reath said, not even trying to hide his broad grin.

"When did you three meet Miss Seton?" Richard asked, pouring himself a much-needed drink from the side table. Without asking, he refilled his friends' glasses.

"Last night at Lady Anson's soiree. Said you couldn't be there due to your lack of wardrobe," Reath said after taking a sip from his drink.

"And absolutely bang on the mark if what you are wearing is any indication of what the rest of your clothes look like," Huntley added.

"Yes, well . . . unfortunately, it does bear a rather close similarity to your wardrobe when you first arrived from the wilds of India," Richard confessed with a teasing grin thrown at Huntley.

"Got to get your tailor here. Can't be seen in public like that," Fungy said, the shock palpable in his voice.

"I'd planned on calling on him today," Richard admitted.

"You mean you were actually thinking of venturing out like that?" Huntley asked, incredulous. "Couldn't you get the fellow here?"

"Yes. Emergency, you know," Fungy added.

"Tell him to bring some half-finished coats with him so you've got something to wear today," Reath agreed.

"And don't forget a few pairs of breeches and pantaloons," Huntley said, nodding.

"Then you can pay a visit to Toby for a new pair of boots," Reath put in, admiring his own gleaming Hessians.

Richard frowned into his drink. His friends were right. He could not go out the way he was dressed. Not the famous Merry Marquis, who had never left the house without being impeccably turned out. He had been out of circulation for so long that he had almost forgotten what was expected of him and his reputation.

Richard sighed and dropped onto the sofa.

"I am sorry, my good friends. I am afraid it has been a long time since I've even thought about any of this."

"Not to worry, Cuz. We'll take care of everything," Fungy said quickly.

"That's right, Merry. You'll get back into the swing of things in no time," Reath said, giving Richard a friendly pat on his shoulder.

"I thank you, all of you, most sincerely for . . ." Richard began.

68   *Meredith Bond*

"No need, no need." "Indeed not! Friends do such things, don't they?" "Really, Merry, don't even think on it." All three cried out in unison.

Richard smiled at them. "Haven't changed a bit."

"No. But you have, haven't you, Merry?" Huntley asked quietly.

Richard nodded sadly. "Yes, I suppose I have."

"Well, not to worry. As we said, we'll get you back to your old merry self in no time," Reath said with authority.

Richard felt a twinge of anxiety. "Must I?" he asked softly, almost to himself.

"Yes, you must" was the definitive answer from all three.

"Owe it to Cousin Teresa," Fungy added.

"Teresa? Oh, dear, I almost forgot about her. You say you saw her at Lady Anson's soiree last night?" Richard drew his brows down again, this time worried not for himself but for Teresa.

"Yes. Had a dreadful time of it too, I'm afraid."

"Cut left and right," Huntley said, nodding.

"I've heard she is rather shy in public," Richard said.

"Shy? You might say she was shy. Trying to hide at every opportunity," Reath said, remembering how Teresa's aunt had to almost physically stop her from ducking behind a pillar the previous evening.

Richard nodded. "I do owe it to her to become my old self again. I'm afraid I did something rather despicable, but I'm going to make up for it." He had a new determination in his voice.

There was an awkward silence. Then Fungy said, "Know all about it. 'Silence' let everyone know."

"Then just marrying her may not be enough." Richard moved to the edge of the sofa, looking intently at his friends.

"A year ago, it would have," Huntley pointed out in his gentle voice.

"But not now." Reath was blunt.

Silence reigned again, but just for a moment. Slowly Reath stood up, his devilish face lightening up into a smile. "Gentlemen, I think it's time for the Merry Marquis to be the darling of the *ton* once again."

"Hear, hear!" Huntley agreed enthusiastically.

"That'll do the trick," Fungy exclaimed.

Richard stood up with determination. "All right, gentlemen. For Teresa's sake, let's get started." He turned toward his cousin. "Fungy, you go to Weston and implore him to be here this afternoon at the latest. He'll listen to you, you've got more credit with him than anyone. Reath, you go to Toby, tell him to get started on a new pair of boots for me, as well as three pairs of pumps. I'll need at least that for all of the dancing parties to which I'll be escorting Teresa. Huntley," he said, turning to the last of the three, "I need you to go with Fungy and help him pick out material for my coats and waistcoats. You now have the most refined taste of us all."

He looked around at his friends. "Gentlemen, I am counting on you. You will be the remaking of the Merry Marquis."

Nine

"Ready to face the wolves, my dear?"

Richard smiled his most reassuring smile at Teresa. He thought ruefully that he could have done with some reassurance himself. It had been too long since he had ventured into a society event. And though Lady Cowper's political soiree was not exactly the sort of gathering that he had normally attended, he was very conscious that it was a crucial first step toward his ambitious goal to restore his own social standing as the Merry Marquis, and, through that, the reputation of his betrothed.

"As ready as I will ever be, my . . . my lord," Teresa said while twisting her reticule strings around her long fingers. This familiar mannerism made Richard realize that she was close to panic, and he took a firm hold of her elbow as they walked into the lovely Georgian town house.

"Miss Seton, Lord Merrick! How wonderful to see you both. I am so glad that you could join us this evening." Lady Cowper's smile of welcome was dazzling as she took Teresa's arm. Then, inclining her raven-curled head at Richard, Lady Cowper added, "My lord, I know that you can manage for yourself. Miss Seton, please come this way. There are some people I would like to introduce to you."

Neither Richard nor Teresa had a chance to say anything before Teresa was gaily whisked away by their most efficient hostess.

As Lady Cowper led her away, Richard could hear her begin to tell Teresa about the people to whom she was about to be introduced. The two ladies were quickly swallowed up by the crowds in the cramped drawing room.

Richard looked around for a familiar face. There were a few men with whom he had a nodding acquaintance, but most were unknown to him. Lady Cowper was known to invite a motley group of people to her soirees. They could be from any class of society as long as they possessed keen minds and an interest in the affairs of the day. There were sallow-faced dons, a cabinet secretary or two with their regal wives, soldiers both retired and in service, and a group of young bluestockings who were deep in conversation among themselves.

Richard sighed, and made his way slowly to the nearest knot of people. Political drawing rooms had never been a fascination of his, nor of Julia's.

Julia. This was the first time he had been out in society since Julia had died. He had never really thought about how much he had depended upon her. She had been the beautiful complement to his dashing good looks, the charm to his wit.

And now she was gone.

Mentally, he shook himself. He could do this. He could go on without Julia. He had to. For Teresa's sake. She was counting on him to help her find a husband.

His mood lightened slightly at the absurdity of the thought, and of his situation. He was going to be Teresa's husband. Yet, he had promised to help her find a man she could love and who returned her affection. He, Richard, certainly did not fit the bill.

Well, he had to do his part. As he joined the nearest group, he forced his mind to focus on the topic being discussed.

"No, it won't last. The French rabble had no great love for the poor king," the man to Richard's left said with great authority.

"You think not? I heard they cheered him like mad," said the man on his right.

"Oh, yes, they will cheer anyone who comes through the gates. But just you wait, the people won't let things simply return to the way they were."

Richard assumed the two were discussing the return of King Louis to Paris. Since Napoleon had abdicated less than a month before, he was sure it had been the most common topic for discussion. There was nothing new that anyone would have to say, and Richard certainly did not have anything novel to add. He moved on.

He passed by three other gentlemen, who were arguing loudly about the American situation. Next was a woman holding forth on the horrors of climbing boys. Her rather bemused audience was an ancient in a wig and diamond-buckled shoes. Amused by the tableau, Richard stopped to listen to her diatribe.

"And so, my lord, I say to you once again, the horrors of mistreatment that is endured by the climbing boys must be stopped, and stopped immediately," she finished as if concluding a major oration to Parliament rather than a discourse to an audience of one.

"Indeed, but then what will happen to the boys? Will you just leave them on the street to starve?" Richard asked mildly.

The woman turned and then looked down her nose at him. "That, sir, is impertinent."

"Not at all. It is a valid concern," Richard said, trying not to take offence at her self-important manner, "and one that must be addressed before any legislation is passed. It would be fine if we establish schools to equip the boys to make a decent life for themselves. But if, madam, you are simply advocating abandoning them to the squalor from whence they come, then you are doing them no service at all."

The woman was held speechless for a moment, but then waded back into the argument. "Indeed, but do you not think that it would be better to fight one problem at a time?"

"But if you are going to fight for the one, perhaps it would be best to fight for the other as a complete solution." The elderly gentleman took up Richard's line of reasoning.

Richard lapsed into a comfortable silence. Listening to the two debate back and forth, he caught pieces of conversation around him as well.

He was amazed at the level of sophistication of the discussions. This was at a much higher intellectual level than anything he had ever imagined would take place at a political salon.

He suddenly thought of Teresa, and how upset she had been the last time she had gotten into a political discussion with someone. Poor girl! She must beside herself with worry about making a *faux pas*. His own uneasiness at being in a social situation vanished as he thought of his betrothed.

Richard excused himself from the argument still raging in front of him. He had to find Teresa.

The room he was in was not very large, but there were quite a lot of people in it. He moved quickly from group to group, looking for her. Growing a bit anxious, he strained to remember the direction Lady Cowper had taken when she had whisked Teresa away.

He walked into another drawing room, even larger

than the first. Once again he moved as fast as possible through the crowd, both looking for her and listening for her voice. She was not anywhere to be found.

Richard truly began to worry. He wondered if she had said something tactless, or had simply been too over-whelmed and had sought refuge in the lady's withdrawing room. A picture came to his mind of her sitting all alone in a room somewhere, crying into her handkerchief.

He redoubled his efforts to locate her. There was no way that she would be able to deal with the intellectual acuity that was present in these overcrowded rooms. Poor Teresa was certainly out of her league here.

He was just about to give up, and try instead to find a lady to look in the withdrawing room for him, when he heard Teresa's voice. It sounded as if it were coming from the far corner of the room. Richard had glanced there earlier, and had seen only a group of gentlemen standing in a tight knot. He had not even stopped to listen to what they were discussing.

He moved toward the group, listening again for Teresa's voice. And then he heard it.

"Lord Southerner, do but consider. A Parliamentary appearance would help all the soldiers. Do you not think that someone would be willing to do that for his own good, as well as for the good of others?"

Richard recognized Southerner as a formidable de-bater he had met during his occasional visits to the House of Lords. His pulse quickened in anticipation of the devastating riposte that was sure to come. Yet, Southerner stroked his chin in thought, and then reluc-tantly agreed. "Perhaps one could be found."

Richard caught a glimpse of Teresa from between two of the men surrounding her. He slowly let out his breath as he noticed that she did not seem to be in any difficulty.

Watching her from the edge of the group, he realized that, in fact, she seemed to be enjoying herself. Her eyes were sparkling with enthusiasm, and she somehow seemed to be using her whole body to convey her point. Her animation reminded Richard of how she looked when she played the pianoforte. He stopped listening to what she was saying, and just watched her.

She was beautiful.

He moved closer to join the group, suppressing the strong urge to pull Teresa from her admirers and drag her home.

To his own home, he realized with a jolt. And what would he do with her once he had her there? The memory of her lips on his just a week before sent his blood racing through his veins.

Her innocence, mixed with a startling passion, had almost undone him. The intrusion by her aunt and Lady Jersey had come at just the right moment. Otherwise, he was not too sure that he could have stopped himself from doing something that they both would have regretted later. As it was, his body still tingled at the thought of kissing Teresa once again.

He dragged his mind away from the feel of Teresa's lips and tried to concentrate once again on what they were saying.

Another of the gentlemen was speaking at the moment. "But I say make the spokesman a peer. A commoner would not have the strength of character to face down the entire Parliament."

Teresa considered this for a moment, furrowing her brow. She nodded, but then changed the focus of the argument. "Yes, a nobleman, then—but because the lords would see one of their own in such difficulties and, just perhaps, would feel some compassion."

Richard was impressed with her reasoning. So where

was the shy young woman his friends had told him about? Or even the awkward and stammering woman he had picked up earlier that evening from Lady Swinborne's house? Here before him he saw nothing but vitality and confidence. This was a woman who knew her mind and who could persuade others to her own way of thinking through eloquence and logic.

"Do you not agree, Lord Merrick?" Lord Southerner asked, drawing Richard farther into the group.

Richard, busy with his own thoughts, had completely lost the thread of the conversation. "I am afraid I must support Miss Seton in this matter, sir," he said diplomatically.

Southerner clearly felt his case was lost. He bowed with a loud creak of his stays and withdrew.

Richard took the opportunity to extract Teresa from the knot of gentlemen so that she might get a breath of fresh air. It was unfortunate, but many of the people present clearly had not begun to subscribe to the modern style of cleanliness. The smell had grown overbearing.

Teresa smiled brightly at Richard as he gently led her toward the open French windows. "Thank you for supporting me."

For a smile like that, he realized with a start, he would do nearly anything. He became conscious that he was simply staring at her. He quickly curved his lips to return her smile and bowed. "I did nothing. It was you and your arguments that won them over. You are very eloquent, my dear."

"Oh!" A pretty pink color stained her cheeks. "I . . . ah . . . thank you, Richard."

"I must admit to you that I was a little worried. I have heard that you've been having some difficulties at parties. Did your aunt not say something about you hiding behind potted plants?" he said, teasing her a little.

Teresa turned bright pink. "Er . . . yes, she might have."

"But you've had no such problems here."

"Oh. No. Well, I suppose it is because I need not watch what I say so closely here. The purpose of being here is to discuss politics, so it is less likely that I will make a *faux pas* than if I were at a ball."

He leaned against the window. "Yes, I understand. But if that is the case, then when at a ball you would do well to remember not to discuss politics. And you would not need to worry about making a mistake on that account."

As a footman passed by, Richard took a glass of lemonade for Teresa and one for himself.

She drained half of it before continuing. "But if I do not talk about politics, what can I discuss? I am afraid that my mother was quite correct. I have no polite conversation."

This was said in such a matter-of-fact way that Richard felt like shaking some sense into her. Instead, he shook his head in frustration and forced himself to speak gently. "Teresa, that is just because you have not practiced. I will be more than happy to teach you what is acceptable conversation at a society event."

Teresa's face lit up at the offer, then fell again. "I believe my aunt tried to do that, but somehow it did not stick. When in company, I could never remember what was allowed and what was not. I would always get mixed up and say the wrong thing."

He laid a reassuring hand on her arm. "Do not worry, Teresa. A few hours of practice with me and you will be charming the pinks of the *ton* with ease."

Teresa looked at him with such hope in her eyes that he felt his heart turn a little somersault in his chest. "Do you really think so?" she asked. "When can we begin?"

"Tomorrow morning. If, that is, you can keep all your new admirers at bay."

The practice session began with Teresa attempting to entertain Richard with idle chatter as her aunt sat nearby with her embroidery. She had started well, though with some prompting from Richard.

They had discussed the weather—it was a lovely spring, despite the fact that, in truth, it still felt more like winter—and laughed over the fictitious decorations at the ball—the Chinese pagoda in the middle of the dining room, with a sphinx inside spouting ratafia into a fountain. But then Richard declared that he would provide no more help and it would be up to her to start a conversation.

Silence reigned for a full minute before Teresa finally remembered a topic of conversation her aunt had told her was impeccable.

"Tell me, my lord, have you recently purchased any horseflesh?" she asked, folding her hands properly in her lap.

"I am so glad you asked that, Miss Seton. As a matter of fact, I have. He is a prime goer and stands at nearly twenty-five hands tall!" Richard said, a broad smile on his face.

"Twenty-five hands! My goodness, how would one mount such a beast?" Teresa could not hold back her laughter.

Richard, too, was clearly enjoying himself. "Why, with another horse, of course. I mount my trusty old gelding roan, Marron, stand up on his back, and from there climb onto my new steed."

Teresa's eyes grew round as she imagined such a feat.

"And please do tell me, my lord, what have you named this fine animal?"

"I have named him Goliath. I felt that to be fitting."

Teresa nodded sagely, hiding her giggles behind the back of her hand. "I see."

Miller, Lady Swinborne's butler, coughed discreetly, interrupting whatever Teresa was going to say next. "My lady, Doña Isabella is here to see you."

Ten

Teresa's mother blew in like a hurricane, complete with water and howls. She stood still for only a moment, in order to locate her daughter, and then burst afresh in torrents of tears and cries of suffering. As she threw herself onto Teresa's neck, she cried piteously, *"Querida!"*

As Doña Isabella began pouring out her woes onto her daughter's shoulder, Teresa could not help but think that she could not remember the last time her mother had embraced her. She also had not remembered how strong her mother's perfume was. Her nose itched and she was hard put not to sneeze. But then she began to listen to what her mother was saying.

Life had been so hard since she left, her mother told her in her native Spanish. It was too much to expect that she could handle everything alone. She could not, so she had sold everything and come to her only child—the only person she had left in the world. She knew that her dear, sweet Teresa would take care of her. It was all that kept her together throughout the long, arduous journey. She knew that her dear, sweet Teresa would take care of everything.

Teresa murmured words of encouragement and strength while her mother cried on her shoulder. Even if she thought she could, she did not attempt to stop the flow of tears.

When Doña Isabella finally ran out of words, Teresa dared to ask the question that had been gripping at her heart ever since her mother entered the room. "Papa?"

This sent Doña Isabella into a fresh wave of tears. Teresa felt her knees collapse under her. Luckily, strong hands guided her back onto the settee.

It was true. He was gone. Her father. The one person who had given her unconditional love and support throughout her life. She thought bitterly of the promise she had made to him to marry for love. What a mockery she had made of it.

Now all she was left with was her mother. She loved her mother very much, but she had finally freed herself, or thought she had freed herself, from the constant criticism she had endured for as long as she could remember. But now her mother was here and there would be no one to buffer Teresa from her harsh words. There was no escape.

Teresa realized that she was now weeping as much for herself as she was for her father. She was ashamed, and immediately began to pull herself together. She had begun to dry her tears with the back of her hand, when a large white handkerchief was pressed into it.

She looked up to see Richard standing next to her. The look of deep sorrow in his eyes almost made her start to cry once more. He understood. Here was the one person who would understand her sorrow, but would he understand her feelings toward her mother? She thought not.

Perhaps her mother would not criticize her if she learned of Teresa's engagement to a marquis. Surely that would raise her up in her mother's estimation? She had to try.

She used the handkerchief in her hand and then turned to her mother, who was still weeping into her own handkerchief. "Mama, please. Mama, you must stop crying now. I . . . I have someone . . . that is, here is . . ."

Doña Isabella sniffed delicately, and turned from her daughter to the man standing next to her. Doña Isabella was the only person Teresa knew who looked even more beautiful after she had been crying, she thought bitterly.

The unshed tears still in her mother's stunning eyes not only made them look larger but also magnified their intense blue color. Her olive skin was slightly flushed, and a few stray blue-black curls had escaped from the knot of hair on the top of her head to frame her lovely heart-shaped face.

"Mama, this is Richard Angles, the M-M-Marquis of Merrick. We . . . we are to be married," Teresa managed to say as Richard bowed to her mother.

"Please accept my most sincere condolences, Doña Isabella," he said smoothly.

Her mother inclined her head graciously. "*Gracias,* my lord." Then she turned to her daughter. "Did you say married, *querida?* You are engaged to marry the Marquis?" she said softly in her beautifully accented English.

Her mother was as predictable as ever. Teresa knew that she would respond to both his title and to the fact that her ugly little daughter, whom she had despaired of ever being married at all, was actually engaged only a short time after arriving in London.

"I am sorry I did not write to properly seek your permission, madam, but I understood that you were busy tending to Mr. Seton's health," Richard said in his deep baritone.

Teresa was afraid for a moment that her mother would succumb to her tears once again, but she simply pressed her handkerchief to her pretty bow-shaped mouth and nodded.

"So good of you to consider my difficulties," she said in a strained voice. "I must admit that I am quite surprised to hear that my Teresita has secured your interest, my lord."

"M-M-Mama . . ." Teresa began, but her mother interrupted her.

"My dearest Teresa." Doña Isabella turned toward her daughter with a look of wonder on her face. "Why, look at you, *mi amor*. It is a good thing I have come. The color of your dress is all wrong for you, and the style is atrocious. Your hair, it does not shine, and you must have forgotten how to put it up as I showed you."

"Mama . . . you . . . you must not . . ." Teresa knew herself to be blushing. She was deeply embarrassed at her mother's criticisms. Her dress was new—the material and design picked out by her aunt. Her hair, too, had been styled by her aunt's own maid. She tried to give her aunt a look of apology.

"Doña Isabella, I assure you, your daughter is one of the most beautiful young ladies of my acquaintance," Richard said with a sweet smile for Teresa.

Teresa could hardly believe it—he was defending her to her mother. No one, not even her father, had ever contradicted her mother.

Teresa looked to see how her mother was taking this. It did not look good. Her mother's beautiful mouth was pulled down, as were her perfectly arched eyebrows.

The scowl lasted only for a second, however, before her mother smiled sweetly up at Richard once again. "Of course she is, my lord. She is my daughter."

Teresa thought she saw Richard's lips twitch with amusement, but he said nothing.

Teresa wondered how such lies came so easily to Richard's tongue. She could never lie, and certainly not to her mother. Her stammers and awkward pauses always gave her away. But Richard was clearly a very accomplished liar. He could lie about his identity, about his whereabouts, and now about her looks.

"Isabella, you must be exhausted. Let me show you to your room." Lady Swinborne, dabbing at her eyes, broke the silence that was about to threaten them.

"Oh, yes, Catherine, my dearest sister. You are so good! Please forgive me for not paying my respects to you. As you could see, I was quite overcome." Doña Isabella took her sister-in-law's hands.

"Of course, my dear. I completely understand. It is quite all right. Come now." Lady Swinborne led Doña Isabella out of the room.

As soon as they had gone, Richard sat down again next to Teresa, who took a deep, shaky breath. It had been an extremely difficult quarter of an hour. It was hard to imagine the emotional upheaval Teresa had just experienced, and she had borne it so bravely.

It was clear that her mother's presence had a large impact on the way Teresa behaved. She had been so happy, with her self-confidence growing as they had conversed easily on silly topics. And then her mother had blown all of that budding confidence out the window with her grand, tear-filled entrance.

In her wake, Richard noted with compassion, she left a stammering, awkward girl who now could do nothing but sit in her silence. Teresa was clearly afraid even to open her mouth for fear of what faltering words would issue from it.

It infuriated Richard to see her thus, and it frustrated him that there was nothing he could do about it.

"My poor Teresa. I am so sorry for your loss," he said quietly.

"Thank you, Richard." Teresa did not look him in the eye but kept her focus on her own hands. "I . . . I am sorry to have used you and your title to impress my mother. I felt I had to do something and I . . . I knew she would respond to it, you see."

Richard tried to coax a smile from her. "I understand. I am glad you were able to make use of my title. I have not often found so many good uses for it myself."

His mild attempt at humor worked, but very briefly.

If only it were now not so very inappropriate for her to come and play on his pianoforte. He knew that that would make her feel better. But he also knew that there was no chance her aunt would let her go to his home alone, and it was unlikely that Lady Swinborne would come along as chaperone. He did not even suggest it for fear of making her feel worse.

Thinking of Teresa at the pianoforte brought to mind the last time he had seen her there. Then, too, her mother had been the topic of discussion, and her insecurities had been at the forefront of her mind.

Richard had kissed away those insecurities. He was very tempted to do so now.

"My mother is very beautiful, is she not?"

The bitterness in Teresa's voice told him precisely how to respond. He made his face as blasé as possible and shrugged. "Yes, I suppose, if you like dark women. I believe that fair skin is much more beautiful."

In fact, Richard had nearly been astounded at the doña's beauty. He knew now exactly what it was that had drawn those soldiers to her drawing room throughout the war. Teresa's mother looked so young that she could have been her sister, and her figure . . . Richard's mouth went dry just thinking about those voluptuous curves. He would never had believed Teresa's mother, or anyone's mother for that matter, could be so desirable.

Teresa's large black eyes looked up at him in disbelief. She could not have looked more different from her mother. And yet there was the same vibrancy in Teresa when she argued or played the pianoforte. Only Doña Isabella somehow maintained her effervescence all the time.

"You are saying that just to make me feel better."

Richard could not resist. He gently stroked her smooth pale cheek with his thumb. "No. If I wanted to make you feel better, I would compliment you on your beautiful eyes, on your perfect face, on your sweet temperament, and on your brilliant mind. But just now I am not sure you would believe me."

"No, you are right. I would not believe you," Teresa said, completely honest as always.

Eleven

Teresa entered the drawing room to find her mother surrounded by three men. She shook her head, dumbfounded. How had they had found out so quickly that Doña Isabella was in London? She had arrived only two days ago.

Teresa was glad no one had noticed her entrance. Just watching her mother and these men converse made her feel tongue-tied. It reminded her vividly of when Doña Isabella had entertained the English soldiers at their home in Madrid.

Her mother, as always, had the gentlemen entranced, hanging on her every word. Teresa wondered how the Doña did it, and why she herself could not do the same thing. Surely it wasn't only that her mother was beautiful? Surely it was also that she was saying something fascinating and enthralling? Why, otherwise, would these men stay at her feet, both literally and figuratively?

One of the gentlemen noticed Teresa's presence and stood. Immediately the other two followed his lead, drawing her mother's attention as well.

"Teresa, finally you have come," her mother said as if they had all been waiting for her.

"I . . . I apologize, Mama, I . . . I did not realize you had guests."

"You remember Sir William, Lord Stowe, and Lord Elybank, do you not?" Doña Isabella said, pointing to each man in turn.

Sir William and Lord Elybank were both exquisites, although Elybank obviously aspired to a higher level of dandyism than Sir William. Lord Stowe, on the other hand, looked more like a fearsome farmer, with a black eye patch covering one eye.

As Teresa curtsied to the bowing men, she vaguely remembered them as visitors to her mother's drawing room before the English army had headed farther north toward France.

"I believe it has been some time, Miss Seton," Sir William said as if reading her mind.

"Indeed, you may not remember us, but I assure you, we remember you, your mother, and your kindness during the war." Lord Stowe smiled at Doña Isabella.

"Yes, yours was a sanctuary amid the chaos of war," Lord Elybank added, making a sweeping bow toward Doña Isabella.

Teresa pressed her lips together and bowed her head, stifling her laughter at this ridiculously ornate speech. Her mother, however, clearly appreciated his words, for she dabbed at her eyes with her lace handkerchief.

"Oh, Lord Elybank, you are too kind. It was our pleasure to be of service to you and the other soldiers fighting for our freedom." She gave her daughter a sharp look before smiling warmly once again at the men. She had seen Teresa's smile.

"I am afraid, gentlemen, we do not have a pianoforte for Teresa to entertain you with here as we did in our home in Madrid," her mother said. "Perhaps, Lord Stowe, you would be so kind as to attempt to converse with my daughter?" Doña Isabella smiled sweetly at that gentleman.

Her mother's taunt hit its mark, and Teresa felt a sharp stab of anger. How could her mother still treat her like a sixteen-year-old? She was no longer an awkward child. Yes, she had retreated into stammering incoherence before, but no more, Teresa told herself firmly. She was a grown woman. She would behave like one and be treated like one. No more hesitations or stuttering.

She took a deep breath to calm her nerves. She could do this. She *could* be witty and charming like her mother, she told herself.

She put on her brightest smile. "You do not need to hide me behind a pianoforte as you did when I was a child, Mother. In fact, I would be delighted to converse with such a distinguished gentleman as Lord Stowe." She then turned to the gentleman in question. "My lord, would you care to sit over there, by the window?"

The gentleman looked awkwardly from mother to daughter, but then said, "I would be honored, Miss Seton."

With a last glance at her mother, who was looking shocked and not a little angry, Teresa led the way to the window seat on the other side of the room.

She could not hide her proud smile. She had done it. She had spoken clearly and without one stutter while in her mother's presence.

Sitting down at one end of the yellow upholstered bench that blended in beautifully with the yellow walls of the room, she gestured for Lord Stowe to take the other end of the bench. Now she had to actually have a conversation with this man.

She overheard her mother say to one of the other gentlemen, "It is dreadful how rude children have become. It is almost as if I never taught the child any manners, to speak to me in that way."

Teresa ignored her and turned her full attention to the

man sitting next to her. She quickly decided that it was merely his eye patch that made him look forbidding. In fact, when she studied the rest of his face, he was almost good-looking, with a gentle aspect. He was not intimidatingly handsome like Richard, nor unusually tall like him, but instead rather average in both looks and height. It must have been his very broad shoulders, chest, and his short, muscular legs that gave the impression that he was shorter than he actually was, Teresa thought to herself.

"How do you find London, Miss Seton?" he asked, breaking the silence.

"Very well, thank you, Lord Stowe. I have been enjoying myself immensely, attending all sorts of *ton* functions." She paused and then cocked her head to one side. "I do not believe that we have met at any of the parties I have been to, have we?"

Lord Stowe's lips twitched as if he were trying not to laugh. "No, we have not. I have recently come from my estate in Sussex."

"It is so difficult sometimes to remember everyone I have met, I am afraid," Teresa quickly explained.

"I understand completely."

Teresa thought that he might. He looked like a very kind man now that his eye patch no longer intimidated her.

She turned the conversation to a topic that interested her more. "How have you been faring since your return from the Peninsula, my lord?" Teresa asked.

His mouth turned down as he took a moment to form his answer, perhaps considering how much to reveal.

Before he had time to say anything, however, Teresa added, "I understand that times have been very difficult for many of the returning soldiers. Even noblemen have not had an easy time of it."

A wave of relief showed on his face. "Indeed, Miss Seton. You are absolutely correct. Things have been very . . . ah, challenging since I returned." He paused.

Teresa nodded. "I have heard that many estates were not looked after as properly as they should have been while their owners were away at war."

Lord Stowe looked startled. "Where did you hear this?"

"I have attended Lady Cowper's political drawing rooms. The plight of the returning soldiers has been a major topic of conversation there," Teresa explained.

Her companion looked relieved. "Oh, yes? That sounds very interesting. You have learned a great deal there, perhaps from other veterans of the war?"

"Yes, there were some gentlemen there who were soldiers. And many more who had wished to be but for one reason or another were unable to join in the fighting."

"I see. So now they are doing what they can for the returning soldiers. That is very good of them."

"Indeed, we all do what we can." Teresa leaned forward and looked intently at her companion. "Would you be interested in helping us, my lord?"

"Me? What could I do?" Lord Stowe asked, startled.

"Oh, you could be of such enormous help to other returned soldiers, my lord. We urgently need a nobleman to plead their case in Parliament. As I am sure you know, my lord, there are not nearly enough jobs for all of the men. Many are living on the streets, unable to do more than beg for their daily bread."

Lord Stowe was frowning, the lines on his face increasing at the picture Teresa was painting. She stopped herself abruptly, aware that she tended to go on too long when it came to discussing the plight of these soldiers.

"Let me understand you, Miss Seton. You wish for

me to be the man who should present their case in Parliament?"

"If you would, my lord," Teresa said, looking at him hopefully.

Lord Stowe smiled ruefully. "No, Miss Seton, I am not sure that I am the right man for this. I have no clout in Parliament at all. I hardly ever take my seat."

Teresa sighed, accepting his reasoning. Yet, he had seemed the perfect candidate, with his frank and gallant demeanor contrasting with the rakish eye patch that testified to his wartime sacrifices. "I understand, my lord, if you cannot do it. Perhaps you could think of someone else who would be willing. Do you think Lord Elybank would be interested?"

Lord Stowe let out a laugh. "No, Miss Seton, not Elybank. I do not believe that such a political speech would be up his line at all." Following his eyes, Teresa looked over at that Exquisite, who was delicately holding Doña Isabella's fingertips while making one of his ornate discourses.

"No, I suppose not," Teresa admitted, sharing his amusement.

Apparently, Lord Elybank's oration was one of farewell. As the other gentleman rose, Lord Stowe, too, stood to join them.

Looking frankly into Teresa's eyes, he said, "Miss Seton, it has been a privilege to talk with you, however briefly. I will think about what you said, and see if I can find someone who would meet your requirements."

Teresa inclined her head, warmed by his compliment, and held out her hand to Lord Stowe. "Thank you so much, my lord, for listening. Please do try, and let me know your thoughts on this matter."

As he bowed over her hand, Teresa could not help but think how easy this gentleman had been to converse

with. He reminded her so much of Richard before . . .
before he had kissed her.

Richard had become such a good friend in the short
time they had known each other, but after he kissed her,
everything had changed. Now every time he touched
her it was like being touched by flames. Her skin
burned and tingled at the contact, and just being with
him made her strangely breathless and very much aware
of his proximity. It made being easy and friendly with
him very difficult.

An appalling thought crossed her mind—if only she
had met Lord Stowe before she had met Richard! Here,
indeed, was exactly the sort of man she had been searching for. He was not too handsome and yet not bad-looking
either, intelligent but not intellectual, and interesting and
easy to converse with. He was definitely someone whom
Teresa imagined she could fall in love with and not feel
overwhelmingly inferior to. And she was sure that his
touches would not burn her as Richard's did. Oh, why had
she not met *this* gentleman before!

The light sensation of his kiss on the back of her hand
nearly made Teresa jump as her attention was pulled
away from her thoughts.

"Once again it has been my pleasure, Miss Seton,"
Lord Stowe was saying.

Teresa felt herself blush furiously, but luckily Lord
Stowe had already moved away to say his farewell to her
mother. "Doña Isabella, I must thank you for the honor
of conversing with your charming daughter. May I be so
bold as to ask if I may call on her again?"

Teresa's mother looked taken aback for a moment.
Then she met Teresa's eye, and turned to smile sweetly
at the gentleman standing before her. "I am so sorry, my
lord, but my daughter will be married in only a few
days."

"Married?" Lord Stowe clearly had not expected this.

Teresa felt herself burn with embarrassment once again. Why had her mother felt the need to tell him this? And why did she look so pleased with Teresa's discomfiture?

"This is Teresa's wedding dress. We had it specially ordered from my modiste. Teresa *should* wear this." Lady Swinborne, her face a little flushed, held up the beautiful white silk gown with the silver net overdress. "She will look lovely in it, Isabella."

Teresa had felt like a fairy princess in that dress when she had tried it on at the modiste's shop. The light flowing fabric of the underdress accentuated what curves she had, while the silver overdress floated around her whenever she moved, giving her an almost ethereal quality.

In short, wearing that dress was the one thing Teresa had been looking forward to in her wedding. The groom made her nervous, sending tingles down her spine with just a look, and she still had not reconciled herself to breaking her promise to her father. She had only to think of the social ostracism that she and her aunt would have to endure if she did not marry the marquis in order for her not to call the whole thing off.

Teresa wished that her mother would relent. One look at her, however, quickly destroyed any hope.

Doña Isabella eyed the dress, distaste written plainly upon her face. "In deference to her deceased father, she will wear the dark blue I chose for her."

"But it does not flatter her as this one does!" Lady Swinborne sounded thoroughly exasperated.

This was the third time in two days Teresa had sat in her bedchamber, watching her mother and aunt have the same argument. Finally, she could not take it anymore. She knew her mother; she would not give up until she had her own way.

Teresa swallowed her frustration and stood. "Aunt Catherine, Mama is right. Out of respect for my father, I will wear the blue." She put her hand on her aunt's arm. "Please, leave it be."

Lady Swinborne's mouth tightened. She looked at Teresa, then at Doña Isabella, and finally gave the dress in her hand to the maid standing nearby. "Return it to the clothespress," she said sadly.

Enveloping Teresa in a warm embrace, she said, "It will be as you wish, my dearest. It is your special day. I only want you to be happy."

Teresa blinked back the tears that started in her eyes. "I know. But unless I do as she wishes, I will never hear the end of it," she whispered in her aunt's ear while Doña Isabella was imperiously ordering the maid to see that the blue dress was properly pressed for the following day.

"Good night, then, my dear," Lady Swinborne said with a final squeeze to Teresa's arm. With a tinge of the rancor she obviously still felt, she wished her sister-in-law a good night as well.

Doña Isabella closed the door behind Lady Swinborne and then turned to her daughter. Her beautiful face was unusually serious. "Sit down, *querida*. There is something I must discuss with you."

Teresa sat on one of the chairs near the fireplace. Nervously, she fingered the tassel on the blue-and-white pillow beside her. She was normally soothed by the decor of the room she had been given in her aunt's house. The upholstery on the chairs and matching coverlet was of a soft azure, harmonizing with the blue fleur-de-lis on the white silk-covered walls. But now the color just accentuated her anxiety at the prospect of a tête-à-tête with her formidable mother.

Doña Isabella sat at the edge of the chair next to hers. She looked closely at Teresa, her large eyes twinkling with mischief. "*Querida,* tomorrow is your wedding day, and there are things you ought to know."

Teresa tilted her head. "Like what, Mama?"

A little smile tugged up one corner of Doña Isabella's lips. "You should know something of what to expect on your wedding night, *querida.*"

"Oh!" Teresa felt her face heat with embarrassment.

Her mother's smile became a laugh. "There is nothing to feel frightened about. I am sure that Lord Merrick will be a very gentle and talented lover."

Teresa flushed again, intrigued yet confused. Doña Isabella leaned forward and continued. "You are surely a lucky girl, *querida.* Why, any man with his broad shoulders, strong legs . . . and his hands, *querida,* his hands—" She stopped, lost in her own thoughts, a small smile playing at the corner of her mouth.

"His hands, Mama?" Teresa was confused. "What is so special about his hands?"

"Have you not noticed? Ah, Teresita, you have a lot left to know! They are large hands, Teresa. And, usually, when a man has large hands . . . well, he is large in *every* way." Her mother's eyes grew round, and she looked like she had just divulged the most wonderful secret.

But Teresa did not understand, and she was not sure she wanted to.

Doña Isabella's tinkling laugh filled the room. "You will learn. And, I am sure, his lordship will be an excellent teacher."

Teresa swallowed hard. The thought of having Richard teach her about the mysteries of married life made her very nervous. Secretly, she wondered what it would be like to see his broad shoulders and strong legs unclothed.

No, she must not think such things. It would never happen. Theirs would be a marriage of convenience. He had said so. It would fall to another man to teach her about the joys of . . . of whatever it was her mother was trying to tell her.

Another man. Perhaps Lord Stowe, or someone else whom she had yet to meet. Suddenly she felt very sad and tired.

"Mama, I am sorry, but I am very tired."

Doña Isabella looked up from her own thoughts, a smile still on her face. "Yes, of course, *querida*. You must get plenty of rest tonight. Tomorrow is going to be a very long and exciting day."

Yes, it was going to be exciting, thought Teresa as she quickly brushed and plaited her long black hair before going to sleep.

Exciting, nerve-racking, and not a little terrifying.

Twelve

Teresa looked in the mirror on her wedding morning and thought again how plain she looked.

Surely, part of the problem was her dress. The dark blue made her skin seem unnaturally sallow and her hair lose its natural brilliance. And although the dress was cut low enough to show a bit of her bosom, the dark hue effectively concealed the rest of her slender curves.

Her mother, overseeing the dressing of her hair, had insisted upon it being pulled up into a tight knot at the top of her head. A few wisps of hair had been allowed to frame her face, and took away some of the starkness. They curled into lovely ringlets.

Even at this time of the morning, the heavy silk of her dress was a trifle too warm, and Teresa felt herself begin to perspire—though, she admitted ruefully, that was probably also due to the panic rising within her at the prospect of the day ahead.

And the night. She would not have given a thought to the night if it hadn't been for her mother's teasing comments all morning long. She felt like telling her mother the truth just to get her to stop her teasing. But that confession would only bring further humiliation. She could not bear that. Not now.

As her maid finished her hair, her aunt came in bearing a small package wrapped in plain brown paper. She smiled a bit tremulously at Teresa, and raised her hand to touch her face.

"Teresa, I love you as much as if you were my own daughter," she said with a catch in her voice. "I wish for you to wear this, as my own daughter would have."

Teresa gave her aunt a tight hug, barely able to contain her own tears. Indeed, she, too, loved her aunt with all her heart.

"Thank you, Aunt Catherine." Teresa sat back down and opened the package. Soft, fine white lace spilled from paper.

"It is my wedding veil. May you be as happy in your marriage as I was in mine." With tears shining in her eyes, her aunt draped it over Teresa's head, allowing the scalloped edges to frame her face.

Looking in the mirror, Teresa felt her first real pleasure of the morning. She heard her aunt breathe, "You look beautiful, my dear."

The white of the veil emphasized her large black eyes and rouged red lips. And, as she stood, it draped down her back and trailed along the floor behind her. Perhaps, she thought as she walked slowly down the stairs, the veil did manage to add a hint of beauty and grace to her otherwise bland appearance.

Her reclusive uncle, the Viscount of Abington, did not seem to notice her attractiveness or lack thereof.

"Pretty little thing," he muttered, tapping her cheek with a finger. But Teresa noted without rancor that there was not much conviction in his quivery voice. He had traveled with great reluctance from his country estate to do his duty by his younger brother's daughter.

Teresa looked down at her tightly clasped hands. It should have been her father who was giving her away. Yet, on second thought, she did not think she could have borne with the guilt of going into a loveless marriage on the arm of her father. No, perhaps it was just as well that it was her stranger of an uncle who would be beside her.

"Are you ready, my dear?" Her uncle offered her his arm.

Squaring her shoulders, Teresa stepped out the door and into the carriage that would lead her to her future husband.

Not her love, but her husband nonetheless.

The butler shut the door behind Richard as he followed Teresa into his town house. The decisive click of the heavy door somehow brought the finality of the events of the day home to Richard. He was a married man again—wed today to this lovely waif who was still very much a stranger to him.

He sat facing Teresa in the drawing room, but then immediately got up again.

For God's sake! He was as awkward as Teresa. He looked over at her sitting uncomfortably at the edge of one the armchairs. She was staring at her tightly clenched hands in her lap, looking so frightened and lost.

He wanted to put her at ease, but oddly enough he did not even know where to begin. Julia would have immediately dispelled the tension with an apt observation, and they would have laughed together. But this girl . . . he really did not know her.

He looked around the drawing room, trying to hit upon something, anything, to say. For a moment he was distracted by the thought that somehow the room looked different with a woman in it. The furniture did not seem quite so heavy, and the walls did not press in on him as they used to when he was here alone.

He took refuge in playing the host. Walking to the

side table where the brandy and a new bottle of ratafia stood waiting, he asked, "Would you care for a drink?"

"No, thank you," she answered quickly. "I . . . ah . . . I've already had more wine than I am used to." She gave him a shaky smile.

"Then I hope you would not mind if I have some." Richard poured himself a generous glass of brandy, then stood there, his back to her, cradling the snifter in his hand.

It was done. The wedding and the breakfast were finally over with, and now he was alone with her. His wife, Teresa.

It still did not sound right. Julia was his wife. Julia, who had been everything to him. God, how he missed her still.

He took a large sip from his drink, reveling in the burning sensation as it slid down his throat.

He turned back to Teresa. She had not moved. There was an odd quality of stillness about her, he reflected, a calm that was very different from the vitality that always came from Julia.

He cleared his throat, knowing that he should say something to break the renewed silence. Dash it, he reflected ruefully, the Merry Marquis being rendered tongue-tied by a slip of a girl—how, indeed, had the mighty fallen!

As he poured himself a second brandy, he wondered about her thoughts now. Perhaps she was remembering their wedding?

He was not sure he could remember much of it himself. His wedding to Julia flashed through his mind. The images were vivid. It had been a grand affair, with the church bedecked with masses of flowers, and sparkling with the so many members of the *haute ton*. Richard's cousin Fungy, with whom he had shared all of the most important milestones of his life, had stood up with him. So had Reath, then newly returned from his diplomatic duties in India and recently married himself. Most of all, he remembered Julia at the altar, her beauty made even more brilliant by the joy in her glowing, smiling face.

And this morning? He remembered Teresa coming down the aisle on the arm of her uncle. And he recalled her dress—the ugliest thing he had ever seen. Yet she had held her head up proudly, and in so doing had caused her beautiful white veil to flow behind her. This, combined with her pale white skin and her flashing black eyes, had given her a fleeting loveliness.

He had heard her speak her vows softly but resolutely, and he remembered the salty taste of her tears when he had kissed her. This was all he could recall.

He walked back to a chair near Teresa and sat down with his drink. Almost at the same time, Teresa stood and moved to the window. She stared out at the street, twisting the maroon damask curtain in her hands.

Looking at her back, he realized that there was one other thing he remembered from that morning. The pain. He remembered the sharp jab of pain when someone had called her Lady Merrick. He had been facing away from her, and had turned instinctively to look for Julia, to drink in her familiar brilliance.

His face must have shown some of the shock and disappointment he had felt on seeing Teresa instead.

She had turned red at his expression but had recovered and greeted her acquaintance with a degree of grace. But remorse still gnawed at him for letting her see his anguish. It must have hurt even if she did not know its cause.

He supposed he ought to apologize, but he just could not bring the words to his lips.

He felt the silence closing in on him. "Would you—"

At the very same moment Teresa turned from the window. "It was quite—"

They both stopped speaking abruptly. Teresa gave a shy smile and said, "I'm sorry, my lord, you were saying?"

Richard quickly took another drink from his glass. "It was nothing. What were you going to say?"

Looking down at the curtain in her hands, she said, "It was not important." She turned back toward the window.

An idea struck him, and he wondered how he could not have thought of it earlier. "Teresa."

She turned and faced him. "Yes, my lord."

He tried to give her his most charming smile. Holding out his hand to her, he said, "Come. Come down to the music room and play the pianoforte for me."

The relief on her face was almost comical. It was as if she had been waiting all this while for him to suggest this one simple thing.

He preceded her down the stairs and to the music room. The fading sunlight made the parquet floor glow red, lending a warmth to the otherwise spare room. The pianoforte had been pulled more into the center of the room, and some gold-covered upholstered chairs arranged casually in a circle in front of the instrument had replaced the gilt chairs. These were much more comfortable to sit in, but Richard had seen to it that two gilt chairs still stood at the keyboard.

With eager anticipation, Teresa sat in her usual chair, pulling a large pile of music onto her lap. All of her music had been brought over with her clothing the previous day, and Richard had had his sister's music brought out and added to it as well, so the pile was a considerable one. She pulled out one piece of music after another, moving it to the top of the pile.

She looked shyly over at Richard, who was sitting so close to her that their knees almost touched. "Would

you like something fast, or slow? Do you sing? There
are some folk tunes or a ballad that we could sing along
with."

Richard smiled. There was still so much they both
had to learn about each other, but her passion for the
music was infectious. He leaned forward, feeling the
warmth of her enthusiasm, and of her body. For the first
time all day, he thought with affectionate amusement,
the real Teresa Seton was beginning to emerge.

No, now she was Teresa Angles. Richard felt his
smile fade and the muscles in his stomach tighten once
again. He was leaning over his wife, whom he had
sworn *not* to touch. Suddenly he felt he was much too
close to her. He shifted his chair farther away from hers.

Her smile disappeared and her face turned pink. "I
. . .I am sorry. Did I say . . . is there something wrong?"

Richard cursed himself. He supposed that in her excitement at being at the pianoforte she had not even
realized that they were so close—or she probably was
not as aware of the moment as he was.

"No. No, not at all. Something faster would be nice.
Something bright. I do enjoy singing, but, if you do not
mind, I will save my voice for another day."

"Yes . . . yes, of course."

Teresa busied herself by picking out a few pieces
from those she had selected and arranged them on the
pianoforte in front of her. Were her hands trembling?

She played through a few scales to warm up her fingers and then launched into a fast rondo by Haydn.

It was obvious that she was nervous. She hit a couple
of false notes, and her pacing was off. He noticed that
she was keeping a close watch on her fingers and the
music in front of her, and was not allowing herself to
lose herself in the music. She must, he thought grimly,
be as intimately aware of him as he was of her.

It was not until Teresa was playing her third piece that she finally began to allow herself to be taken up by the music. It was a more flowing piece that she was playing, and he was not sure if she was actually reading the music in front of her or playing it by heart.

Her eyes were mostly closed, and her body moved with the fluid melody. A small smile rested on her lips, and her pale face glowed with the love of the music she was creating. Richard watched, enthralled with her beauty, slowly losing himself as well. Her calm and the beautiful music filled him with peace. The tension of the day melted away, and Richard felt that they were both able to relax finally. Within minutes Richard almost felt as if the chaotic past few weeks had not happened at all.

He sat forward in his chair, ready to turn the page, when she reached across him for a key at the far end of the keyboard. With the feel of her body's heat, even momentarily against his, he was forcibly reminded once again that this was their wedding night.

He wondered what she was expecting. He had promised not to touch her, but would he, could he, hold himself to that promise? Despite having moved his chair away, her proximity was still almost overwhelming to his senses. Her scent and the warmth that radiated from her body reminded him of a field of lavender in summer.

He had not realized how difficult it was going to be to know that she was his wife and yet he could not touch her. He felt the tension in his body mount. Let him just make it through this evening. Perhaps it would get easier after that.

"Are you finished, my dear?" Richard said from his end of the table.

This was ridiculous, Teresa thought to herself. There

were just the two of them, and yet they sat at either end of a long table in the formal dining room.

She was not used to eating in state. She and her aunt had been quite informal when it had been only the two of them. They had been served by just the butler, not the four—or was it five—footmen. And that was in addition to the footmen who stood behind their chairs in case they should desire anything at any moment.

Was this part of being a marchioness? Her aunt was only a baroness. Perhaps, as one moved up the ranks of the nobility, everyday life got more formal?

She wondered if she could ask that her place be set next to his in the future. She was the mistress of the house now, but perhaps Richard would be hurt if she tried to change things. No, she was still too unsure of her position in his house to suggest it.

Besides, from where she was sitting, there was no way for her to suggest anything to him. The only way for them to speak to each other was by shouting across the expanse of the dining table. Although perhaps that was deliberate. She wasn't sure of what she would say to him were she by his side.

Teresa eyed the huge urns next to the oversize fireplace that took up a large portion of the wall to her left. The mantelpiece was covered with carved fruit, vegetables, and vines of grapes, which wound their way around the fireplace and up the wall to the high ceiling. There they intermingled with sheaves of wheat and farming implements, which decorated the four corners of the ceiling. An impressive chandelier hung from the center of the ceiling with hundreds of carefully polished pieces of cut glass reflecting the light of the candles. The walls were painted a deep green and covered with paintings of food and farming to complete the theme of the room.

Teresa shook herself from her woolgathering to answer her husband. "Yes, thank you, my lord. Shall I retire and allow you some time with your port?" She rose from the table as she spoke, and the footman behind her jumped to pull her chair back from the table.

Richard stood as well. "No. That is not necessary. We need not stand on ceremony when it is just the two of us."

Given her thoughts of a moment earlier, Teresa found this very funny. Unwittingly, she let out a laugh.

Richard smiled at her, wanting to share the joke. "What is so amusing?"

"How can you say that we should not be formal, when we have had a most formal dinner, sitting at either end of a table meant for twenty, and being served eight courses, most of which we did not touch? Is that not standing on ceremony?"

Richard looked back at the table as they left the room and laughed. "You are correct, my dear. Although the table was actually designed to seat thirty," he said with a twinkle in his eye. But immediately he grew more serious again. "Perhaps tomorrow you can speak to Samuel, and he will be sure to set your place next to mine."

So, she *could* make changes. That was good to know. She felt slightly more at ease, until she looked back at Richard as he followed her up the stairs to the drawing room. He had pulled his eyebrows over his eyes and he held his back stiff and erect. A moment before, he had laughed with her. Why was he now frowning?

Almost as soon as they had entered the drawing room, Samuel came in with a note for Richard. Upon reading the note, he looked up at Teresa with a little smile, or was it a look of relief that had crossed his face?

"I am so sorry, my dear. It seems that I need to go out on an urgent matter. I hope you will excuse me."

Teresa did not know what to make of this. He had to go out? Now? On their wedding night?

"Yes . . . yes, of course." What else could she say?

He gave her a little pat on her shoulder. "There is no need for you to wait up for me. I do not know when I shall return." He headed out the door with a light step. "Good night, Teresa."

"Good night," she said to the closed door, for her husband had already gone.

Teresa looked about the empty room. She was alone in a strange house on her wedding night. She blinked back the tears that burned her eyes and took a deep breath. There was no reason to stay here, she thought, and rang for the housekeeper to show her to her room.

Things were still not quite right. Richard stared at the amber liquid in his glass as he sat back in the worn leather chair in his library. His orphanage still had a few problems that needed to be worked out. It seemed like each time he fixed one problem, immediately another would take its place.

Finally, the staffing problem had been fixed, but now the tutors needed more help. It was their note that had come to him just after dinner. They had written to respectfully request a few minutes of his lordship's time.

Richard almost laughed out loud at how he had jumped at the request like a drowning man at a rope. It had been exactly what he needed—to get away from Teresa. The smile faded from his lips.

Richard stood and began to pace the room. He stopped and stared out at the empty street through the window.

The moment he had seen the smile on Teresa's face and heard the laughter in her voice, he knew he would not be able to hold on to his tenuous control if he stayed in her presence much longer. He had been relieved to have the excuse to get away from his enticing new wife. He had never been so grateful for Samuel's penchant for formality as he had been that evening. The farther he stayed from Teresa, the easier it would be to keep his promise.

Returning to his chair and his drink, he forced his mind back to the orphanage. Julia would have been so pleased with the way it was working out. It was just as she had wanted it to be. A grand house, more like a home, filled with boys who had never known the meaning of the words *home* or *love*.

She had loved children, and they had looked forward to having quite a few of their own. It never came to pass, however, and then she was gone. His thoughts of what would have been hurt almost more than the pain of her absence.

Tomorrow morning he would go to spend time at the orphanage, as he liked to do. And he would interview more tutors. It would be pleasant to spend a day in the company of the boys, whom he enjoyed. And more important, it would be a day away from Teresa.

He got up again to refill his glass and then rested his elbow on the mantelpiece, staring down at the flames in the fireplace.

It worried him that Teresa enticed him so much—it made him uncomfortable. He loved Julia and missed her so much that sometimes he could barely stand the pain. That he should have such thoughts about Teresa angered him.

But she was so close by. Just upstairs, asleep in Julia's bed . . . And what disturbed him even more was that Teresa was here too, in his mind.

Richard allowed his eyes to focus on the carpet at his feet. The stain was still there.

A blood-red stain on his white carpet. He remembered the exact moment it had happened. He had been sitting in his chair, contentedly reading and sipping a glass of wine, when the footman had come in with news of Julia's death. His glass had fallen from his nerveless hand.

Although he knew they had tried, no one had been able to remove the stain.

Richard stared at the carpet, the familiar grip on his heart tightening. Perhaps it was just a trick of the candlelight, but somehow the stain looked less vivid than it had been.

Thirteen

Teresa was surprised when her maid informed her that she had a visitor.

"Please inform his lordship, and tell him that I will be down in a moment," she told the maid, who was still standing at the door, waiting for instructions.

"But his lordship has gone out, my lady."

Teresa was stunned. "Gone out? Where? When?"

"I . . . I don't know where, my lady. He went out just after . . . after ten this morning." The maid had gone pale at Teresa's expression.

Teresa stood still, absorbing this unexpected news. "He didn't say when he'd be back or where he was going?"

"No, ma'am."

"All right. I'll be down shortly," Teresa said with as much calm as she could muster.

As soon as the maid left, Teresa began to wring her hands and pace back and forth. What was she going to do? Lord Stowe was downstairs, waiting for her. He had probably come to pay his respects to the newly married couple. The problem, of course, was that the bridegroom wasn't here. How was she to convince anyone that she was happily married when her husband wasn't at home on the morning after their wedding!

She realized she was beginning to panic. She stopped her pacing and tried to calm herself.

It had been difficult enough this morning to wake up all alone in a strange room. She had looked across the huge expanse of her bed and wondered what it would have been like to awaken in the arms of someone she loved. She had hugged a pillow to her chest but had cast it away after only a minute. It had been a poor substitute.

And now she had to face this, this abandonment, once again. Only now it would be a rejection in the presence of others.

Teresa felt her despair beginning to turn to anger. How could he do this to her? How could he just leave her to face visitors on her own? She started pacing furiously once again. Why could he not at least have had the courtesy to tell her that he was going out? She supposed that he was used to living alone, and neither of them had even thought that they would have visitors on this very first day after they were married. She hoped that he would have stayed if he had known.

To have to entertain guests was frightening enough, but to have to do so in Richard's house all alone . . .

No, now it was her house too. She had to remind herself of this. It still didn't feel right, but she knew that this was the only way to think if she was to behave naturally.

Teresa checked her appearance to make sure she looked the part of the blissful bride. But the plain girl staring back at her from the glass bore little resemblance to a happy new wife. She frowned at her image and then squared her shoulders, pulling her lips up into a smile. Well, she was going to have to pretend.

As she entered the drawing room, she saw that Lord Stowe was not alone. Her mother was there as well. She groaned inwardly.

Lord Stowe stood at her entrance and bowed with a rather sad smile on his face. "My felicitations, Lady Merrick," he said by way of greeting. Despite herself, Teresa

We'd Like to Invite You to Subscribe to Zebra's Regency Romance Book Club and Give You a Gift of 4 Free Books as Your Introduction! (Worth $19.96!)

If you're a Regency lover, imagine the joy of getting 4 FREE Zebra Regency Romances and then the chance to have these lovely stories delivered to your home each month at the lowest price available! Well, that's our offer to you and here's how you benefit by becoming a Regency Romance subscriber:

- **4 FREE** Introductory Regency Romances are delivered to your doorstep (you only pay for shipping and handling)

- 4 BRAND NEW Regencies are then delivered each month (usually before they're available in bookstores)

- Subscribers save almost $4.00 every month

- You also receive a **FREE** monthly newsletter, which features author profiles, discounts, subscriber benefits, book previews and more

- No risks or obligations...in other words, you can cancel whenever you wish with no questions asked

Join the thousands of readers who enjoy the savings and convenience offered to Regency Romance subscribers. After your initial introductory shipment, you receive 4 brand-new Zebra Regency Romances each month to examine for 10 days. Then, if you decide to keep the books, you'll pay the preferred subscriber's price, plus shipping and handling.

It's a no-lose proposition, so return the FREE BOOK CERTIFICATE today!

Say Yes to 4 Free Books!
Complete and return the order card to receive this $19.96 value, ABSOLUTELY FREE!

If the certificate is missing below, write to:
Regency Romance Book Club
P.O. Box 5214, Clifton, New Jersey 07015-5214
or call TOLL-FREE 1-800-770-1963
Visit our website at www.kensingtonbooks.com.

FREE BOOK CERTIFICATE

YES! Please rush me 4 Zebra Regency Romances (I only pay for shipping and handling). I understand that each month thereafter I will be able to preview 4 brand-new Regency Romances FREE for 10 days. Then, if I should decide to keep them, I will pay the money-saving preferred subscriber's price for all 4...that's a savings of 20% off the publisher's price. I may return any shipment within 10 days and owe nothing, and I may cancel this subscription at any time. My 4 FREE books will be mine to keep in any case.

Name _____

Address _____ Apt. _____

City _____ State _____ Zip _____

Telephone ( ) _____

Signature _____ RN082A
(If under 18, parent or guardian must sign.)

Terms and prices subject to change. Orders subject to acceptance by Regency Romance Book Club.
Offer valid in U.S. only.

felt a little warmed at how sad he looked. Perhaps it was because he knew that she was now unavailable for him to woo.

"Thank you, my lord. It was very kind of you to come." Teresa forced herself to look Lord Stowe in the eye, and to ignore her mother's searching look at the doorway behind Teresa.

Her mother spoke up even as Teresa dropped a light kiss on her cheek. "*Querida,* but where is your beloved husband?"

"I am afraid he had to go out early this morning," Teresa replied, moving over to the bellpull to ring for some tea.

"Ah." Doña Isabella winked at Teresa. "I knew he would be a strong and vigorous husband. Even after the rigors of last evening, that he still had the energy to go out and attend to his usual activities says a great deal about his fortitude."

Teresa felt herself burn with embarrassment, her hard-won composure about to desert her. She was not entirely sure why, but she knew that her mother was hinting at something improper. Even Lord Stowe had turned quite red.

Teresa was never more relieved to hear Lady Cowper's name than she was just at that moment. Although grateful for the diversion, she hoped her confidence in her friend not to reveal to her mother that she and Richard had been forced to marry was not misplaced.

"Lady Cowper, how wonderful to see you," Teresa said, taking that lady's hands.

"Lady Merrick, I do hope you will excuse the intrusion, but I simply had to come and offer you my heartfelt felicitations." Lady Cowper gave Teresa's hands a friendly squeeze.

"Thank you. Have you met my mother? She has recently arrived from Spain."

Just as she had hoped, Lady Cowper immediately engaged her mother in conversation, leaving Teresa free to devote her attention to Lord Stowe.

"I expect you had quite a busy day yesterday," he said as Teresa sat near him.

"Yes. It was." Teresa paused, twisting her fingers in her lap as she wrestled with finding the right words to convey to him the awkwardness of her situation of being married to one man while still seeking to fall in love with another. Looking down at her hands, she said, "My lord, I do hope that my marriage will not affect our friendship."

"It is up to your husband, of course, but I, too, hope that we may continue to be friends."

When Teresa dared to look up into his eye, she saw that he was smiling warmly at her. She was greatly relieved to see that smile. There was still hope.

"Have you thought any more on who I might ask to represent the soldiers in Parliament?" Teresa asked, steering the conversation to a more neutral subject.

Before he could answer, Doña Isabella interrupted him. "My lord," she called out in her charming accent, "you were going to tell me about this marvelous actor you saw upon the stage. What was his name? Kay?"

"Kean, Doña, Edmund Kean. Have you see him, Lady Cowper?" Lord Stowe asked, effectively passing the conversation off to her.

Teresa wanted to laugh at her mother's expression as she was forced to listen to Lady Cowper go on about Kean's performance at the theater.

A gentleman had never turned down her mother's attention in favor of her own, and she could tell by the rather forced, bitter smile on her face that her mother was not pleased.

Teresa interlaced her fingers on her lap and leaned toward Lord Stowe as if she were sharing great confidences.

"No, Lady Merrick," he was saying. "I have not thought of anyone yet. But, since you had asked, I am still thinking about it daily."

"You are very good, my lord. I am certain you will discover someone we can ask. Surely you know many of the other officers who fought in the Peninsula. Is there not one who has returned and could speak for the common soldier?"

"I am afraid, as yet, I have not come up with anyone. Have no fear, we shall think of someone."

There was an awkward silence for a moment as Teresa desperately tried to think of some other exceptional topic of conversation. In a moment of inspiration, she remembered her practice session with Richard just before her mother's arrival. She hid a giggle behind a cough and then asked, "My lord, have you bought any horseflesh recently?"

"Why, yes, as a matter of fact, I have."

Teresa could not contain herself. Remembering Richard's invented horse, Goliath, she began to giggle.

Lord Stowe gave her a confused look. "I am sorry, Lady Merrick, but what is so amusing in purchasing a horse?"

"Nothing at all, my lord, I assure you," Teresa said, trying to contain her mirth. "It would not happen to be a very large animal, would it?"

"No. I suppose it is an average size for a horse, about twelve hands high. Why?"

Teresa coughed and tried to stop herself from laughing. "Oh, I see. Well, Lord Merrick and I once discussed the purchase of horseflesh and he—oh, dear, there is no way to explain this. I am so sorry, my lord. I assure you, I am not laughing at you, but rather remembering this other conversation Lord Merrick and I once had," Teresa said, giggling all through. She stopped and took a deep breath, finally managing to control herself, but Lord Stowe was still looking a little bemused.

"My lord," Doña Isabella broke in to their conversation once again, "I do hope that you are planning on attending Teresa's wedding ball?" She batted her eyelashes at Lord Stowe while giving him a smile.

"Yes, of course, Doña Isabella, I would not miss it for the world," Lord Stowe said. He turned back to Teresa. "Lady Merrick, do you expect quite a lot of people at your ball?"

"I believe that my aunt is hoping that it will be the event of the season. As she and my mother have been making all of the arrangements for it, I do hope, for their sake, that it is well attended."

"We have received a flattering number of acceptances," Doña Isabella said. "In fact, I do not believe that anyone has turned down their invitation."

"No one would turn down an invitation to see Merry," Lady Cowper stated.

"I would hope that no one would turn down an invitation issued by myself and Lady Swinborne," Doña Isabella announced imperiously.

"I should hope that no one would turn down an invitation to meet Lady Merrick either." Lord Stowe winked at Teresa, who suddenly found herself blushing furiously.

"Well, I am sure that is merely crude curiosity on the part of society." Doña Isabella dismissed Teresa with a wave of her hand.

Teresa opened her mouth at the injustice of this, but

Lord Stowe beat her to it. "I am sure that society *is* curious to meet the lady with such address as to catch the attention of the Merry Marquis."

Doña Isabella opened her mouth to retort to this statement, but then suddenly stopped herself.

Teresa could barely believe it. Lord Stowe had stopped her mother's harsh words. This was the second time she had seen her mother contradicted. The first had been Richard, and now Lord Stowe.

Oddly enough, her mother did not look as if she minded Lord Stowe contradicting her as much as she did when Richard had done it. In fact, she had an odd look on her face. One of curiosity and interest. But how could she be interested in a man who was refuting her, albeit gently? That certainly was not possible.

Still, Teresa was very thrilled that Lord Stowe had defended her.

"Do you expect your husband to return soon, Lady Merrick? I had hoped to pay my respects to him as well," Lord Stowe asked.

The maid entered with the tea tray, and Teresa busied herself with pouring out the tea while avoiding Lord Stowe's eyes. Her former embarrassment at Richard's abandonment returned with force. She had actually completely forgotten about it until Lord Stowe reminded her.

"I do not believe he will be gone too long, my lord." He had better not, she added silently to herself.

"Lord Huntley, my lady," Samuel intoned with authority.

Teresa looked up to see Richard's friend enter the room. As with nearly every time she had seen him, Lord Huntley had a large smile spread across his brown face, showing off his perfectly white, even teeth.

Teresa could not help but return his smile as she

stood to welcome him. "Lord Huntley, how very good to see you again."

He bowed over her outstretched hand. "My dear Lady Merrick, it is good to see you looking so happy. I trust you are well?"

"Yes, indeed. You remember my mother, Doña Isabella, and Lady Cowper, of course. And this is Lord Stowe, a friend of mine."

After shaking hands with Lord Huntley, Lord Stowe said, "I suppose I shall have to wait to meet Lord Merrick another time. Thank you so much, my lady, for your generous hospitality." He then turned to Teresa's mother. "Doña Isabella, would you do me the honor of allowing me to escort you home?"

A smile spread across Doña Isabella's face, and with it a look of triumph as well. "Yes, of course, my lord." She stood and gave him her hand in a most slow and graceful fashion.

Teresa saw them to the drawing room door. "Thank you, my lord, for coming to visit me. I do hope you will come again very soon," she said, and then turned to her mother. "Mama, please give my love to Aunt Catherine." She kissed the air next to her mother's cheek.

Teresa felt very happy. Lord Stowe was going to prove a good friend to her, she was sure. He was very kind and entirely set her at her ease. Unlike Richard of late.

As she was handing a cup of tea to Lord Huntley, she looked up to see her husband entering the room.

He strode in with a broad smile of welcome on his face. "My profound apologies, my dear, I did not realize we would have visitors so early."

"Indeed, my lord. I am happy you have come." Teresa felt a wave of pleasure roll through her. It was just relief, she told herself. She was angry with him, but at least she would not have to be embarrassed by his absence any further.

Richard took Teresa's hand, and with a twinkle in his eye, gave it a lingering kiss.

She felt the familiar burn at the back of her hand where his lips had touched it. The heat ran all the way up her arm and then into her face as she felt herself blush. She suddenly realized that her mouth was open. She closed it with a snap and then swallowed hard.

Richard raised an eyebrow at her reaction, and then turned to greet the other guests with aplomb.

Teresa leaned back in her chair, collecting herself, and watching Richard work his charm on Lady Cowper, who was positively glowing at his attentions. It would be impossible for any female to resist that charm, Teresa thought, trying to defend herself for forgiving him so easily.

Fourteen

Richard knocked on Teresa's door. "Teresa, come along, we will be late," he called through the door.

The door opened to reveal her maid.

"Where is . . . her ladyship?" he asked, peering into the room over her shoulder.

"I am sorry, my lord. She is in the drawing room, waiting for you. Has been this past quarter of an hour." The maid curtsied to belay her rudeness.

"She is?" Richard was shocked. Both Julia and his sister had always taken a long time to dress. He had assumed all women did. He went down to the drawing room.

When he opened the door, he felt as if the wind had been knocked out of him. There stood the most beautiful woman—his wife. She was dressed all in white and silver. A silver cloth with pearls sown onto it was wound around her head, holding her hair up and away from her face, while the rest of her long black hair fell in graceful curls down her back.

"You are beautiful." The words came from his mouth before his mind had registered them in his brain.

She blushed. "No, but it is kind of you to say nonetheless."

"If I did not mean it, I would not have said it. You look beautiful this evening, Teresa." He came farther into the room and gently took her fingers, which had been tying themselves up in the strings of her reticule.

She looked down at their hands. "Thank . . . thank you, my lord."

Richard took his first breath since he had walked into the room. Somehow his heart felt too tight in his chest. "Do you know that you have not called me by my name since we've been married?"

She looked up, her large black eyes wide with wonder. "I am sorry, I felt that that would be rather . . . rather intimate."

Richard wondered if she would prefer not to be intimate with him at all. He supposed that she would not. For some reason this hurt him more than he wanted to admit, even to himself.

He forced himself to smile. "We are married, Teresa, we are supposed to be intimate. No one else knows that ours is merely a marriage of convenience. Shall we, at least, try to give others the impression that we are happy?"

Teresa turned toward the window so that Richard could not see her face. "Yes, of course, my . . . Richard." Her voice was very soft, almost hoarse. For a moment Richard wondered if she was trying not to cry, but he quickly dismissed that idea when she turned back to him with a smile on her face.

"We should go, or else my mother and aunt will wonder where we are," she said in a much stronger voice.

Richard held out his arm for Teresa to place her hand on and then led her out to their waiting carriage.

Richard spent the journey trying not to think about the fact that his wife would rather be married to someone else, or not married at all. Instead, he tried to focus on the upcoming evening. Since his foray into the social world at Lady Cowper's, he felt more confident, but still not fully comfortable about reentering society without Julia. Tonight he would be meeting all of his old friends and acquaintances. It was surely going to be a difficult evening.

He was determined, however, to make it a good one for Teresa. She needed to get over her anxiety about going into society if she was ever going to find anyone she actually wanted to marry.

Just before getting down, Richard took Teresa's hand once again. "I do hope you are not too nervous," he said gently.

Teresa peered through the darkness into his eyes. "Somewhat. Are you?"

"Yes," he admitted. He was surprised at himself. He had not known that he could acknowledge such a thing out loud, but once it was said, he felt much better about the coming evening.

Teresa's fingers gave his a reassuring squeeze. "Then we shall both just have to be the merriest people there."

Richard laughed. "Well, I am the Merry Marquis. Will you be my Merry Marchioness?"

Teresa took a deep breath. "Yes, and I will do so without discussing politics," Teresa said boldly. But then Richard heard her say to herself, "I hope."

The hall Lady Swinborne had rented for the ball was resplendent with glittering chandeliers and glittering people. It seemed as if all of London wanted to be present at the coming-out of the Merry Marquis and his new bride.

Teresa's face hurt from smiling so much, but finally her aunt had allowed that it was time to move away from the door and open the ball by dancing the cotillion with Richard.

Teresa moved over to where Richard was talking with a group of gentlemen. They were all laughing at some witticism one of them had made. She supposed it had been Richard, as the man standing next to him slapped him on the back and said, "You are still the same, Merry. It is a shame you have been hiding yourself away for so long!"

Richard's face took on a sad, serious look for a moment, but then his eyes met Teresa's and he gave her broad smile.

"Gentlemen, my lovely bride." He stepped back to allow her to join the group.

"I . . . I am terribly sorry, my lord, but . . . but we have been instructed by my aunt to begin the ball," Teresa managed to say, fully aware that all eyes were on her.

But Richard's eyes were warm and kind as he looked down at her. "Of course, my dear, I would be honored." She felt heartened by his look and took his arm, allowing him to lead her out for the dance.

Afterward, Teresa was relieved that she had been asked to dance by a number of gentlemen, since it made it unnecessary for her to worry about making much conversation beyond the weather.

She watched from the corner of her eye as Richard danced and laughed with one lady after another. She was amazed at his ability to simply walk up to someone and within moments have her smiling and laughing along with him. He had even done so with many of the shy young women who lined the walls, looking awkward and sometimes downright scared.

Teresa supposed that she had looked that way, too, at many of the balls she had attended. But tonight she had not even had a chance to stand still for two minutes, she was so sought after. It was an odd occurrence, and one that she entirely put down to the fact that she was now married to Richard.

She took advantage of Lord Stowe's request for a dance to take a break and ask him to bring her some refreshment. She had dared not do so with any other gentleman for fear of not remembering any appropriate topics of conversation, but with Lord Stowe she felt comfortable enough that she did not need to worry.

As she stood waiting for him to return with her glass of lemonade, she could not help but overhear the conversation going on just behind her.

"Oh, indeed, it is such a shame," said a voice that sounded familiar.

"I have heard that she was very beautiful," said another hesitantly.

Teresa turned her head so that she could see out of the corner of her eye who was speaking. Her suspicions were confirmed. It was the Diamond, Miss Bowden-Smyth, and Miss Peyton talking. She remembered them well from one of her morning visits to Lady Jersey's. The Diamond had been insulting Miss Peyton when Teresa had intervened and turned the tables on her. But now it appeared that they were in agreement about something. Teresa strained to hear more of their conversation even though she knew that she should not.

"Lord Merrick's first wife was the toast of the town the year before last, and I believe that she was considered an Incomparable for a few years before that. Not only was she very beautiful, but very charming and witty as well," the Diamond said with great authority.

"What a lovely couple they must have made."

The Diamond clucked her tongue. "As I said, it is such a shame. It must have been the shock of losing his wife, but to have come down so far as to marry Miss Seton is just beyond all comprehension. Why, she is such a graceless provincial. He must be horribly embarrassed by her this evening. That would explain why he is keeping his distance from her."

Pain and anger sliced through Teresa. She knew now there was only one thing she could do—prove the Diamond wrong.

There was a silence for a moment, and Teresa turned to see Miss Peyton staring directly at her, her face bright red with embarrassment. The Diamond, however, was also looking straight at her, only with a slight sneer on her face. Teresa lifted her chin and looked the Diamond straight in the eye. "If you think that I care one fig for you or your spite, Miss Bowden-Smyth, you can think again. In fact, I believe you are simply jealous because I have married the most eligible and handsome gentleman of the *ton*."

Teresa intercepted Lord Stowe as he approached with her lemonade. After drinking deeply from her glass, she took a long breath, put on her most charming smile, and began to talk with him in the animated manner she had seen her mother assume. She forced herself to be both charming and witty and even attempted to will herself to be pretty.

She could tell that Lord Stowe was rather surprised at first, but then a smile spread across his face as he was completely taken in by her ruse. Soon he was laughing along with her and hanging on her every word, just as he did with Doña Isabella. Teresa could hardly believe it.

She caught Richard looking at her from across the room with a strange expression on his face. It was sort of a mixture of awe and confusion. He gave her a reassuring smile and then moved on, she supposed, to find his next dance partner.

Unfortunately, when Teresa's next dance partner came to claim her hand, she was completely unable to maintain her charade. Suddenly, with a new person, she was thrown off her stride and fell back into being her old nervous, awkward self. She tried to fool herself into thinking that this gentleman was as friendly and inclined to think well of her as Lord Stowe obviously did, but it did not work. She simply looked at the gentleman escorting her to the dance floor and felt all of her good resolve crumble to dust.

Richard forced himself to behave normally. Although his strongest desire was to avoid everyone and everything and seek out a quiet corner where he could mourn his beloved Julia, he knew that he could not do that. He had spent most of the past year doing very little besides thinking about Julia and how much he missed her. Now he had to stop thinking of her and start thinking about Teresa. This was not too difficult, since Teresa was in such desperate need of his help, and he had never been able to not help someone.

He had watched her stammer out her greetings to everyone who had walked into the ball, trying to lend her his support in every way he knew how. He even went so far as to make sure that she had plenty of dance partners for later on that evening.

Still, it had been a painful experience for both of them. He was made fully aware of what it must feel like for people who did not have the social ease that he had always taken for granted. Greeting people, he had to search his mind for witticisms and compliments that had always come so naturally to him. For the first time in his life, he had to work hard to maintain his Merry Marquis facade.

After doing his duty by escorting a number of ladies, both young and old, to the dance floor, he managed to escape outside for a breath of fresh air and a moment of quiet. He had known it was going to be difficult without Julia, he just hadn't realized how hard it would be to maintain this persona that everyone expected from him. What had once come so naturally was now a struggle.

"Lovely evening."

"My, it is hot in there."

It was Fungy and Julian. Richard turned to look at his two friends. "Where is Sin?" he asked. Although not pleased to have been found, he was relieved it had been his closest friends who had done so and not anyone else.

"Reath is dancing with his wife, of all people." Fungy gave a theatrical shiver of disgust. "I've tried to tell him again and again that it is unfashionable to do so. Refuses to listen."

"Well, as you see, I am following your advice," Richard said, holding his laughter in check, "as is Julian."

"Yes. Thank goodness you two have some decency," Fungy sighed.

"Lady Merrick does not seem to be having any trouble finding partners," Julian commented.

"I've worked damned hard to make sure of that," Richard said dryly.

"Done an excellent job." Fungy patted Richard on the back. "You seemed to be rather busy on the dance floor yourself."

"Yes, for much the same reason as Teresa. It is much easier to dance than to have to stand about, making insipid yet witty conversation."

His friends stood silent for a moment. A blatant look of shock on Fungy's face, but then he schooled his expression into its normal bored look. "You are always witty, Merry. Trying too hard. Just be yourself."

Richard nodded at the wisdom of this. Perhaps he had

been trying too hard. He was out of practice and felt the weight of his obligation to Teresa.

After returning to the ballroom, Richard did as Fungy had suggested. He tried harder to relax and just allow his innate social ease to take over. And after some time he stopped, amazed and pleased that it did seem to be working.

He deliberately sought out ladies whom he knew he needed to pay special attention to—the patronesses of Almacks and the other leading hostesses from whom Teresa would need invitations. And he allowed himself to follow his natural inclination to dance with the wall-flowers. As he fought the urge to simply join them in their silence, he figured he would do better asking them to dance instead.

He also had to force himself to keep from looking around for Teresa too many times. The first time he saw her, she was dancing with Lord White. She looked nervous but managed to give her partner a smile as the movements of the dance brought them together. Richard felt sorry for her but knew that there was nothing he could do but to continually supply her with dancing partners so that she need not worry about making any *faux pas* in conversation.

The second time he saw her, however, was much later in the evening. He was surprised to see her speaking with a gentleman with an eye patch whom he did not know. That she knew this gentleman well, however, was obvious as she stood laughing with him. Richard had never seen her so animated except when she was discussing politics. But he did not think she was holding such a discussion now because she did not have the same intense expression on her face as she did when she was concentrating on an argument. Richard stood still, watching her.

No, the more he thought about it, the more she

looked just like her mother when she was entertaining a gentleman. He was confused as to how Teresa had suddenly discovered this hidden ability of hers. When their eyes met, he gave her a smile. She turned back to her conversation and Richard went searching for Lady Swinborne. He had to find out who this gentleman was whom his wife was so comfortable with.

Instead of finding her aunt, Richard discovered Doña Isabella talking with an older gentleman with a great mustache.

"Lord Stillwater, have you met my new son-in-law, the Marquis of Merrick?" Doña Isabella asked as Richard walked up to them.

"No, I do not believe I have had the pleasure," the gentleman replied, bowing to Richard.

"Lord Stillwater is one of our heroes of the Peninsular War, Merrick," Doña Isabella began.

"Oh, no, Doña, I can lay no claim to any heroism. I was simply another officer," the gentleman said, blushing slightly and huffing into his mustache.

"And a modest one too." She smiled coyly at Lord Stillwater.

Richard motioned toward Teresa. "Doña, do you know the gentleman your daughter is speaking with?"

Doña Isabella followed the direction of Richard's eyes. She looked rather surprised for a moment, as she, too, noticed how animated Teresa was being and how enthralled Lord Stowe was with her. But then a slow smile returned to her face. "That is Lord Stowe. He is also a Peninsular War hero. Did he not serve under you, Lord Stillwater?"

The gentleman raised his quizzing glass and peered in Teresa's direction. "Yes, yes, he did. Stowe is a fine young man, and an excellent leader."

Richard asked, "Then you and Teresa met him when he was in Spain?"

"Yes. And, of course, he has come to visit Teresa on numerous occasions since she has been in London. Why, he was at your house just the other day. He came to pay his respects to her on the occasion of your marriage, I believe."

"He did? Teresa did not mention it to me." Richard was beginning to wonder just how close his wife and this Lord Stowe were. If she had met him as many times as his mother-in-law was implying, then perhaps Teresa had a strong interest in the fellow. Perhaps that was why Teresa had been so sure that she did not want to marry him. Perhaps she wanted to marry this man instead. Richard felt his heart tighten in his chest.

He thanked Doña Isabella for the information, then went off to do his duty to his next dance partner, but it was with much less enthusiasm than he had had previously.

Richard was pleasantly surprised to find Teresa in the same set as he and Miss Bowden-Smyth. As they came together in the exchange of partners that was part of the country dance, the look of wonder and happiness on Teresa's face when she saw him lightened his heart considerably. However, they were each forced to return to their original partners, and he watched as Teresa returned to being the awkward woman he had seen most of the evening.

"It is rather embarrassing for you, I suppose, is it not, Lord Merrick?"

Richard was startled by the voice in his ear, and turned to see Miss Bowden-Smyth looking rather smug as she followed his wife with her eyes.

"I am sorry. What is embarrassing?" he asked, not liking either the tenor of her voice or the look on her face.

"Why, the fact that you had to marry an antidote like Miss Seton. Just look at her, she has absolutely no grace whatsoever and looks rather like a frightened deer with those huge black eyes of hers."

Richard looked back at his wife. She did indeed seem frightened with her large eyes so wide open as she looked up uneasily into the face of her partner. "She is just a little nervous, that is all. It is much better to be ill at ease than too high in the instep, don't you think, Miss Bowden-Smyth? No man likes a hoyden," he said, looking down his own nose at her.

The Diamond had the grace to flush, and retreated into silence for the rest of the dance.

"You looked like you managed to enjoy yourself after all," Teresa said in the carriage on the way home.

"Yes, I must admit that it was much more pleasant than I had thought it would be," Richard agreed.

"I'm glad that you found it so."

"You also danced almost the entire evening," Richard said.

"Yes. It was certainly much easier than trying to actually talk with anyone," Teresa admitted.

"Poor Teresa. You are still worried about that. I had hoped that you were more confident now."

"Well, perhaps I am a bit more confident."

"I am sure that you are. I saw you laughing with a gentleman with an eye patch, what was his name?" Richard asked, a slightly hard edge to his voice.

"Lord Stowe. But he is a friend," Teresa said, wondering if Richard would be upset if he knew that she had entertained hopes of marrying Lord Stowe.

"Ah, yes. You seemed to be very comfortable while speaking with him."

An awkward silence fell over them. The carriage pulled to a stop and the steps were let down.

Richard followed Teresa into the house but then stopped her as she began to mount the stairs to her room.

"I will say good night to you here, Teresa," he said, putting his hand on her arm.

She turned around. Standing on the first step, she was nearly as tall as he and could look directly into his deep green eyes. There was something there, some sadness or hurt. But it was gone almost immediately, making Teresa wonder if it was simply a reflection of her own feelings she was imposing on him.

"Oh? Very well, then. Good night, my lord," Teresa said, quickly looking away so that he would not see the hurt in her eyes. She supposed that she was simply tired after the excitement of the ball. There could be no other explanation for the way she was feeling.

He ran a finger along her jawline, forcing her to look up into his eyes once again. He wore a rather sad smile. "Good night."

Very quickly he turned and walked away. She watched him go into his library and close the door behind him.

She continued up to her room, where she undressed and slipped quickly into her overly large bed. Holding her pillow to her chest, she quietly wept herself to sleep.

Fifteen

As the powerfully melodic song flowed effortlessly from the large woman standing at the front of the room, Teresa leaned forward at the edge of her chair, intent. Richard was impressed as well, but he had heard Signora Capellini sing before and so was not as enthralled.

Lady Thorpe's musicales were very well regarded among the *ton*. She always managed to get the best musicians and singers to perform for her "little get-togethers." It was, therefore, a rather overcrowded drawing room in which they sat in closely placed chairs—latecomers, being not so lucky, were forced to stand around the walls of the room. Richard desperately wished someone had had the forethought to leave some windows open, as the room was getting rather warm and close.

And, of course, an evening at Lady Thorpe's would never be complete without a performance by her extremely talented daughter. Evangeline Thorpe was, unfortunately, not very pretty to look at, with her small eyes and her pinched face framed by mouse-brown hair. However, once she began to play her harp, it was easy to forget her looks and to merely sit and enjoy the beautiful music. Her long, graceful arms reached around her instrument, plucking and stroking the strings to produce the most lovely, flowing melody.

Richard looked over at Teresa with a smile but found

her rapt once again. Unconsciously, her eyes had half closed and her body was swaying slightly with the music. She seemed to be letting the music permeate her being rather than just hearing it. Richard had a hard time keeping his eyes from her. He gave up the battle, enjoying the music not just for its own beauty but for the lovely effect it had on his wife.

The three selected pieces were played, and fervently applauded by all. Lady Thorpe then stood up and said, "And finally, we have one more performance for you this evening." Lady Thorpe looked around. "Lady Merrick, would you be so kind as to come up?"

Teresa jumped, her eyes going wide. "Me?"

Richard smiled at her and gave her hand a squeeze. "Go ahead, Teresa, you play so beautifully."

"But I . . . I haven't prepared anything."

Lady Thorpe laughed. "Oh, I am sure you are very well prepared. Please, Lady Merrick." She gestured to the pianoforte that was being pushed forward by two footmen.

Richard stood up to allow her to pass. "You will be wonderful. Don't worry, my dear," he whispered as he pulled her into the aisle.

Nervously, Teresa made her way to the front of the room. She gave Lady Thorpe a quick smile. "Thank you," she whispered as she seated herself at the pianoforte.

As always, she had dressed beautifully for her society visit; but in her absorption with the performances during the course of the evening, she had become slightly disheveled. Some of her hair had come loose from its tight chignon, and Richard noticed her fingers tremble as she quickly fixed her coiffure.

An uneasy hush had fallen over the room as the assemblage realized how uncomfortable she was. Richard felt his own nails digging into his palm as they all waited for her to begin.

Teresa raised her hands over the keyboard, and, after a false start, launched into a slow and melodic piece by Haydn. Richard let himself relax as the music began to flow from her fingers—perhaps not as effortless as usual, but still pretty enough.

And then she missed a note.

And a few more. Her mistakes continued to get worse until she stopped altogether, seemingly paralyzed and unable to go on.

Richard felt his stomach tighten. He, as well as everyone else in the room, watched her as she sat with her eyes tightly closed, fighting her demons.

There was a hum, and even a few titters from some of the girls in the audience. Richard could clearly hear Miss Bowden-Smyth, who was also present, say in a stage whisper, "Not only is she boorish when you speak to her, but she can make a fool of herself at the pianoforte too."

Richard felt himself flush with anger, and was about to turn around and deliver a stinging set-down, when his eyes were arrested again by Teresa. She had clearly heard the comment as well, for she had turned bright red. But at the same time, she visibly shook herself and started again.

This time, instead of continuing with the slow Haydn piece, she launched into one of the fast and very complicated pieces by Soler that she favored.

She was brilliant. There was no other word for it.

Richard watched, spellbound with the rest of the audience, as Teresa's fingers flew up and down the keyboard at a pace so fast that they almost blurred. The music swooped and soared around them, the virtuoso performance filling the entire room with bold and sparkling notes that blended into one another.

The piece ended quickly, but its memory still hung in the air during a prolonged moment of astonished silence. Immediately thereafter, the stillness was shattered by an outburst of applause and bravas, and calls for more.

Unable to suppress the broad smile on his face, Richard joined in the applause. As Teresa took her curtsy, he caught her eyes for a fleeting moment and was delighted to see a small glint of a smile reflected back at him. The applause died down as she sat and began to play once more.

It was the Haydn piece again. Only this time it came out beautifully, with no hesitations or mistakes. Teresa had finally begun to relax and play the way Richard knew she could. Within a few minutes she became totally lost in her own music.

Richard watched, fascinated as always, as Teresa began to glow and move with her music. A small smile played upon her lips and, even from where he was sitting right in the middle of the room, Richard could see her half-closed eyes framed by her long black eyelashes.

Without pause she played one more lilting piece before remembering where she was. She stood up, flushed with her exertions and obviously embarrassed to have so completely lost herself in the music.

The applause was fervent. To Richard's ears it seemed louder and more heartfelt than for any of the previous performances. As Teresa tried to make her way back to Richard, she was stopped again and again by people complimenting her on her recital.

Richard stood and watched as she went from being rather awkward at first to flushing with pleasure and finally to conversing easily with all of the men and women surrounding her. Smiling to himself, Richard left her to her admirers and moved away to get himself a drink.

At the refreshment table Richard ran into his cousin Fungy.

"Inspired, Merry old man," Fungy said, patting him on the back.

"She is very good, isn't she?"

"Yes, 'course she is. I was, however, referring to you."

"Me?"

"Obvious you put her up to it, m'boy," Fungy said, giving Richard a sly half-smile. "Don't deny it."

Richard laughed. "No, I don't. I knew that Teresa would enjoy a musicale. It is the first one we have been invited to. I could not help but jump at the opportunity." He took a long drink from the lemonade in his hand and then helped himself to a lobster patty.

"I had hoped that the more parties Teresa went to, the easier they would get. Unfortunately, this has not proved to be the case," Richard said.

"Had some moderate success at your wedding ball," Fungy offered, trying to give Richard a little encouragement.

"Yes, she did have a few moments there when she forgot to be self-conscious, but more often that not she simply went through the motions of social conversation with all the grace of a frightened deer."

"Suppose it makes escorting her rather trying," Fungy said sympathetically.

Richard nodded and tried not to show his cousin just how close to the truth he had come. Teresa's lack of composure and self-confidence made escorting her to social events a strain, a stress compounded by his own periodic urges to escape.

Yet he did have to admit to himself that he was finding it easier to slip into his Merry Marquis persona with each party they attended. But this simply meant that while Teresa stuttered and groped for something to say to the few people who approached her, Richard's group of admirers, both male and female, was growing. It was awkward when many of those who sought him out were old friends expecting Teresa to be another Julia. Their disappointment when it was discovered how awkward she was was evident.

"Still," Fungy said, helping himself to more lemonade, "have to admire Teresa's efforts."

"Oh, absolutely. And we practice her conversation as often as we can. But the problem is not that Teresa does not have conversation. She has proven herself to be confident and capable when we attend Lady Cowper's political drawing rooms. When she is completely focused on the point she is making she doesn't think about being self-conscious or awkward. I believe playing the pianoforte does the same thing. She is so focused on her music, she forgets everything else. I was sure that this would work, and it has, hasn't it?"

"In spades. Never seen anything like it. Just look at her."

Richard turned around to look, and realized that he couldn't see Teresa because of the crowd of people, mostly men, surrounding her. He could hear her laugh, however, and answering chuckles from the group, and knew that she was holding her own in the crowd.

Fungy's chortle caught his attention, and he turned to look at his cousin. "What is so amusing, Fungy?"

"You, dear boy. Should see the scowl on your face." His cousin's lips twitched again.

"I am not scowling," Richard denied vehemently. How could he be irritated at Teresa's social success when he had just explained to Fungy that this was entirely his intention? Why would he be scowling just because his wife was completely surrounded by a bunch of young and eligible tulips of the *ton*? Was that

Hawksmoor holding Teresa's hand? Now, he was a rogue of the worst sort.

"Jealous. That's what you are." Fungy interrupted Richard's scrutiny of the gentlemen surrounding his wife.

"I most certainly am not jealous." He was, however, rapidly becoming very annoyed with Fungy. He walked away.

Richard had not wanted to get in Teresa's way, but he could not resist the urge to be near her. He found himself making his way through the crowd to stand by her side.

She was glowing, still. Whether from her performance or from all the compliments and flattering words being heaped upon her from the gentlemen surrounding her, Richard did not know. All he could see was that she was more beautiful than ever.

Very soon, to his relief, the crowd began to disperse.

"You seem to have quite a number of new admirers," Richard said after the last one had walked away.

"Yes, I suppose I did," Teresa said, still feeling rather exhilarated from her sudden success.

She had been surprised by the amount of attention she had received after her performance. Never had she had such an experience, not even when she had performed for the soldiers at her father's house in Spain. But here, by the way they crowded around her as soon as she had finished, it was as if they had never heard anyone play the pianoforte before.

And then there had been the compliments.

"You were absolutely brilliant, Lady Merrick," Lord Millhaven had said, taking her hand and kissing it.

A redheaded young dandy she had met only once before and could not now remember his name gently pulled her hand from Millhaven's grasp to place his own salute on it. "Never have I seen anyone more beautiful at the pianoforte than you, dear Lady Merrick."

Teresa opened her mouth to refute him, when Miss Peyton joined them. "Lady Merrick, that was an incredible performance. I never knew you could play the pianoforte so well."

"Th-thank you, Miss Peyton," Teresa managed to say. Teresa could easily set aside the gentleman's compliments, but for Miss Peyton to say that she had done well truly meant something to her.

"You really think I was good? I was so nervous at the beginning."

"That was certainly obvious, but then once you truly began to play . . ." Miss Peyton began to say.

"Once you started to play, Lady Merrick, you were magnificent," the unnamed dandy finished for her.

"Indeed, and not only played superbly, but were lovely to watch as well," Lord Millhaven added.

Other gentlemen who had crowded around her seconded this statement.

"You are all too kind," Teresa said.

But somewhere deep inside her, Teresa had felt a spark of pride begin to grow. And with it came self-assurance. She did not understand how it was happening, but the more compliments she received, the easier she found it to talk to all the people around her. Before she knew it, she was laughing and having fun and not feeling self-conscious at all. She had forgotten to be nervous and shy.

They spoke of music and the performances by Signora Capellini and Miss Thorpe. Teresa praised them both as wonderful artists. More than one gentleman who had begun to say that Teresa was so much better changed their tune when Teresa insisted that they were equally good, if not better than she. They were so eager to please her and to agree with her that she nearly laughed.

When Richard joined the group, at first she had been happy to have him next to her. He added to her sense of well-being and comfort. But then he began to give such fierce and angry looks to the gentlemen who surrounded her that very soon they all moved on, and she was left alone with Richard.

"Why did you frown at them all so?" she asked him.

"Frowned? Did I? I am sorry, I did not mean to scare them away. But, honestly, Teresa, you could do better than Hawksmoor, Millhaven, and Crusty Corstairs."

Teresa laughed, "Crusty Corstairs? Is that what the red-haired gentleman's name is?"

Richard finally smiled. "Yes, did you not know? I am certain you've met him before."

"I had, but I could not remember his name." Teresa laughed again. "Oh, dear, now I'm sure I won't forget it."

Sixteen

After returning home that evening, Richard bade Teresa good night at the bottom of the stairs as usual, and then quickly retreated into his library before he was tempted to act on his growing attraction toward her. However, for some reason, even as he sat down in his favorite chair, he felt the urge to go out.

He hadn't actually been to his club for some time, preferring the solace of his library to continuing with the effort that was still required to maintain his merry facade. This evening, however, he wanted company.

The smoke-filled room at Whites was gratifyingly unchanged, with the same heavy leather furniture scattered about the large reading room. Richard walked through on his way to the card room, which in turn was filled with the same tables that had been there for as long as anyone could remember. Also unchanged was the acrid smell of tobacco mixed with the sweet smell of alcohol and the sometimes pungent odor of unwashed male bodies. Richard suppressed a laugh as he thought that it would probably be this way even a hundred years from then.

He found Fungy at a card table with lords Riverton and Kelter, the fourth seat having just been vacated. Richard was pleased to make up the fourth in their game, and ordered a bottle of brandy for the table.

They had barely begun the bidding, when Lord

Riverton said, "Hear your wife had quite a night, Merrick. Didn't realize she was a pianoforte virtuosa."

Richard could not hide his smile, and the glow of pride that had suffused him for most of the evening returned in full force.

"She is normally very quiet and shy, is she not?" Lord Kelter asked.

"Yes, normally," Richard answered.

"Not tonight. Had nearly every young buck at Lady Thorpe's surrounding her after her performance," Fungy said in his usual succinct manner.

"Heard Lady Thorpe wasn't too pleased about that." Lord Wold joined in the conversation, standing next to Richard and peering down at his hand of cards with his quizzing glass.

"Had rather high hopes for that sour puss of hers, I imagine," Lord Riverton replied.

There were some appreciative chuckles from other gentlemen who were watching the play unfolding on the card table.

"Oh, I don't know. I suppose she's not much to look at, but Miss Thorpe is a very nice, even-tempered girl," Richard said in her defense.

"Easy for you to say, Merrick, you don't need to worry about being caught in the parson's trap," said a young gentleman standing to the left of Fungy.

"Doesn't it bother you, Merry, that your wife was completely surrounded by so many young fribbles?" Lord Kelter asked.

"Of course it does! Did you see the card he just played?" another gentleman answered before Richard could say anything. There were guffaws of appreciative laughter from the men surrounding them.

Smiling, Richard watched Lord Riverton neatly stack the pile of coins in front of himself. He had better try harder to concentrate on his cards, he thought while dealing out the next hand.

An hour later his purse was considerably lighter, but his mind was completely relieved of any anxiety over Teresa's performance that evening. Richard thanked the other gentlemen at the table and stood. He knew when to cut his losses and was too well aware that it was not the cards that were holding his attention that evening.

Fungy followed his lead, and the two were soon joined by Huntley and Reath in sharing a bottle of port in front of a slowly ebbing fire.

Julian lifted his glass. "Here is to Teresa's success."

"Hear, hear!" Fungy and Sin chorused.

Richard, too, lifted his glass. "And to her continued success."

"Yes, and what shall you do for an encore, Merry?" Reath asked, sipping appreciatively at the excellent wine.

"Why, I need not do anything. She has all the invitations a girl could want. Now I am just going to sit back and relax and let her take over."

"Do you think she'll be able to?" Julian asked, sitting forward in his chair.

"I certainly hope so. I can't say that I've exactly enjoyed dragging her around to all of these routs and balls every night," Richard admitted, his high spirits coming down a step.

"You haven't? Always enjoyed them before." Fungy was clearly surprised.

"With Julia, yes, I suppose so. But now . . ." Richard stopped, feeling a lump forming in his throat.

"Merry, Julia's been gone for over a year," Julian said gently.

"But that doesn't mean that I've forgotten her." Richard could not keep the hard edge from his voice.

"No, of course not, but you have Teresa now," Reath said.

"Yes, and because of her I've had to reenter a social world I was living very happily without." Richard poured himself another drink.

"Just don't understand that one, Merry. You've always been an out-and-outer," Fungy said, shaking his head.

Julian agreed. "Fungy is right. Even if it weren't for Teresa, you still should be social, Merry. You should be attending parties for yourself."

Richard looked at his friends who all sat around him nodding and agreeing with one another. They just did not understand how much he missed Julia. How vital she had been to him. He could not be himself without her, it didn't feel right. He just didn't think it was possible. But his friends did not understand, and he did not know how he could ever explain it to them.

"You have got to live your life not just for Teresa, but for yourself," Reath repeated in his deep, commanding baritone.

Richard sat back in his chair and looked Reath in the eye. "It sounds easy when you say it, Sin, but how am I to do it? I've been living alone for a year, and I must say, I've gotten rather used to it. I'm not as comfortable in society as I was when I was with Julia. I don't know that I can do it without her."

"But you can. I don't know how, I just know that you've got to," his friend insisted.

"Seen you do it, old man," Fungy said, filling up Julian's glass and then his own. "I have seen you being your merry old self at numerous parties."

"That was not me. It was an act," Richard admitted.

Reath let out a laugh, "Well, if so, you should be on-stage. Do you remember Princess Lieven's face when you asked her to dance the waltz the night before last?"

Richard, Fungy, and Julian all burst out laughing as they remembered the horrified expression that lady had given Richard and the supreme set-down he had also received from her.

"Thought she was going to have apoplexy!" Fungy said, trying unsuccessfully to stifle his laughter.

The other men only laughed harder.

"Whatever made you ask her for the waltz?" Julian asked, wiping the tears of mirth from his eyes.

"I just wanted to see what she would do," Richard said, and then burst out laughing again. "She still hasn't spoken to me, but at least she hasn't given me the cut direct."

"Well, once again you're the ape-leader, Merry. Now every young buck wants to try asking the older matrons to dance the waltz," Reath said.

"The betting book is filled with wagers on who will succeed first and with whom," Fungy added.

"Oh, no! I honestly didn't mean to start that. But it was a lark, wasn't it?" Richard said as the laughter died down.

Julian took a restorative sip from his drink. "Yes, and not only that, but it was just like your old self, Merry, wasn't it? You are not going to say that that was an act, are you?"

Richard looked at him and felt the smile fade from his face. "No, it wasn't. I suppose I have had my moments, haven't I?" He had done it without thinking, just for the fun of it. It had felt good. It had felt right.

"You see, you can still do it. You can be your old self. But for some reason when you realize what you are doing, you stop," Reath said, coming directly to the point.

"Can't run and hide every time you begin to have fun, Merry," Fungy added.

Richard looked around at his friends. "No, but it's certainly easier that way."

Unfortunately, Richard began to realize that his friends

were correct. He had to stop running away from life. He had to allow himself to be the Merry Marquis. He had to do it for Teresa and he had to do it for himself.

He sat forward in his chair again. Raising his glass, he proposed a toast. "To the return of the Merry Marquis?"

His three good friends raised their glasses and chorused, "To the Merry Marquis!"

Teresa looked across the tea tray at her husband and tried to stop her giggles.

They were sitting in the drawing room, attempting to practice being in a formal situation, but Teresa just could not keep a straight face. It was a good thing she did not play cards, she thought to herself.

She noticed Richard trying to suppress his own smile as well. "Teresa, you cannot burst out laughing every time you discuss buying a horse. I assure you that to a gentleman, the purchase of horseflesh is a very serious topic."

Teresa put a hand over her mouth to hide her smile. "Yes, Richard, I will try to remember that."

"Very well. Now, shall we continue?"

"Oh, but, Richard, I cannot think of how to continue this conversation. Really, I cannot," Teresa said, putting down her teacup and beginning to fiddle with the fringe on the pillow next to her. Despite her giggles, she was becoming truly worried that she would make a complete fool of herself that evening.

She still was unsure of how she had so totally lost her self-consciousness the previous night at the musicale. That she had been able to laugh and talk with so many men and women all at once still confused her.

Was it merely the compliments on her performance, or was it the topic of conversation? Music was one thing she knew very well, and that was the main thing she had talked about.

And yet she had also been quite proud of herself for having played so well and having been able to lose herself in her music in front of a large audience. Yes, that was it.

When talking, she had been able to hold on to that feeling she had when she lost herself in her music, except it was conversation and wit she had lost herself in.

Richard's voice cut into her thoughts. "Well, if you are truly in need of inspiration, you can perhaps try looking about you. Remember, you will be at a ball. Why don't you comment on people's dress or the decorations as we have done in the past? Such trivialities can carry conversation quite well."

"They can? Well, then that does make things easier. I can do that, I believe," Teresa said, relaxing slightly and moving the pillow behind her back, where it belonged.

"Yes, of course you can, my dear. Don't worry, you will be fine . . . as long as the subject of returning soldiers doesn't come up!"

Teresa answered Richard's twinkling eyes with a rueful smile of her own. As she did so, she realized how much easier it was to converse with Richard when he was a little distance away. Having him too near seemed to cause her some difficulty with her breathing, and her thoughts too somehow became distracted.

She had been in a great deal of difficulty the other night after they had returned from a soiree. Instead of saying good night to her at the bottom of the stairs as he had been doing for the past few weeks, he had followed her up to her room. Teresa had worried that he was going to follow her into her bedchamber itself. Luckily, he had stopped just short of that.

She had no idea what she would have done if he had wanted to . . . to . . . What *would* he have wanted to do?

Exercise his rights as her husband? What would that entail? The thought sent a rush of warmth through her body.

"Teresa, you are woolgathering again!"

"What? Oh, I am sorry, Richard. I was trying to think of what I might comment upon this evening," Teresa lied. Lying was becoming easier for her, she realized with chagrin. She was lying to society about the true state of her marriage, and she was beginning to realize that she was lying to herself about her growing feelings for Richard.

She had convinced herself that she was happy with the fact that Richard had not entered her bedroom so far. Yet, in the middle of the night, when she lay awake all alone in her huge bed, she would wonder about what was missing from her marriage. Only then did she admit that the feelings she held for her husband were growing beyond the platonic relationship they had agreed upon.

But that was as far as she would admit, even to herself.

She looked at Richard's handsome face, which now held a look of affectionate concern.

"Are you worried, Teresa? Don't be. I have full confidence that you will think of something at the right time." Richard stood up and put his teacup back onto the tray. "But I am afraid, my dear, that I must leave you now. I have some work I must attend to."

Teresa rose as well. "Thank you, Richard, for taking the time to do this with me."

Richard turned to her before moving toward the door. "Of course, my dear, it is entirely my pleasure. You will go and amaze your admirers this evening, I have full confidence in you." And with a flash of his brilliant smile he left the room, leaving Teresa a trifle weak at the knees— at the prospect of having admirers she would need to amaze, she told herself sternly.

Seventeen

That night at Lady Debenham's ball, Teresa shone. Just as she had the previous night at Lady Thorpe's musicale. When surrounded by her admirers, she somehow forgot her fears. She laughed and glittered, and was flattered and feted.

The die had been cast very soon after they entered the ballroom.

"Oh, what a lovely gown, Lady Jersey! Such an unusual color, but it suits you admirably!" Teresa's remark made Richard stiffen and turn to her half in warning. The gown was an unfamiliar shade of brown, a color he did not particularly like on women.

"Do you really like it, Lady Merrick?" Lady Jersey slowly appraised Teresa, causing Richard's heart to quicken some more. But Lady Jersey clearly saw the honest admiration in Teresa's face, which brought an answering smile to her own.

"It is a new color, called Devonshire brown—after the color of the soil there. See, if you look closely near the light, you can see the reddish highlights," Lady Jersey continued, taking Teresa's arm and drawing her under a chandelier. This boded very well for the rest of the evening, Richard thought with some relief.

Soon after "Silence" had made her rounds, Richard was hearing compliments about Teresa's sweet and honest nature as well as about her beauty and talent. The word had spread, and ladies and gentlemen alike sought out this new paragon.

Somehow tonight, just as she did at the musicale, Teresa forgot her shyness.

Although she still had moments of awkwardness, Richard was pleasantly surprised by her newfound ability to forget to be shy and awkward. Every so often, as the crowd and conversation thinned, she would look to Richard, clearly hoping for conversational inspiration. If he was nearby, he would take matters in hand and make some witty comment about the cut of a gentleman's coat or the plethora of flowers that adorned the ballroom. Teresa would laugh, regain her confidence, and carry on the thread of the conversation without her admirers noticing the slight lapse.

He was, at these times, amazed that he, himself, was able to help her out so easily. Her need of him made it so much easier to be the Merry Marquis that there were times when he barely thought about it.

He knew that he, too, still had moments of uncertainty, like Teresa. It was at those times that he wished more than anything that he could go home to the solitude of his library. But then he would look over at his wife and feel a rush of delight in seeing her doing so well. If she can do this, then so could he.

His pride in Teresa, however, was tempered by a dull ache around his heart that was somehow more intense when Teresa was at her social best. Richard wondered if it was because the more his wife shone, the more likely it was that she would be able to find a match and free herself from her imposed marriage.

No, that was a ridiculous thought, he told himself as he stood there in the crowd, watching her throw her

Meredith Bond

head back in laughter at the wit of a rather handsome, dark-haired young Corinthian.

The whole point of their marriage had been for her to maintain her social standing despite being compromised, and for him to help her find a man she could love. Perhaps one of the bucks surrounding her at this moment?

If so, he told himself, she could do better. But that was not the cause of the pain, he assured himself. No, this ache was due to the fact that her ability to converse with ease was growing by leaps and bounds, and soon she would no longer need him to help her at all.

And it certainly had nothing to do with Julia, he realized with a start. In fact, he had not thought about her the entire evening. A familiar stab of guilt slipped between his ribs, adding to the pain that had started at the sight of Teresa with her beaux.

A folded fan rapped him lightly across his shoulder. He turned to the pretty blonde who was trying to claim his attention. Here was something to keep his mind from his unpleasant musings.

"Ah, Lady Margaret, how enchanting you look this evening." He forced a smile onto his face as he brought her hand to his lips.

The young lady was dressed in willow green, bringing out her bright green eyes. Matching green jewels twinkled from her blond hair, which was twisted into a complicated knot on top of her head.

"Why, you are like a wood nymph in that lovely color," Richard added approvingly.

Lady Margaret flushed a pretty pink. "You do not think me a bit too green, my lord?"

"Oh, no, my lady, no one who knows you would think you are too green," Richard replied with a twinkle that brought an answering flush to her cheeks.

Without pursuing his *double entendre,* he continued

smoothly. "No, indeed not. You look like a nature sprite. Like a breeze on a summer's day."

And she smelled like one too, Richard thought as he leaned closer to her in his bow. Unfortunately, the smell was more of a field studded with sheep rather than one strewn with flowers. But she was lovely and charming, and Teresa was clearly busy.

"Would you honor me with this dance, Lady Margaret?"

Lady Margaret held out her hand for him to take, and Richard led her out into the set that was just being formed. He managed to keep his distance from her through the dance, so as to not have to smell her, but had to stay close enough to periodically voice witticisms to her to keep her entertained.

Despite his partner's charms, Richard's eyes kept straying to find Teresa. She presented an exotic and alluring picture in her new dress. It was a pretty shade of rose that accentuated the color in her lips and cheeks, and her hair cascaded in ringlets around her face. Her dress was cut low, showing a beautiful expanse of white flesh, which drew many a gentleman's eye. And she was even more incredibly, ethereally lovely when she was enjoying herself as she was now.

Once again he realized that his body was betraying him. Over the last few days it had been increasingly difficult to hide his growing desire for her. The more time he spent with Teresa, the more he wanted her. He knew it could never be. He had promised her that theirs would be a marriage of convenience, and he could not betray her trust.

And yet, the other night, he had almost followed her right into her bedroom, catching himself just at the last minute. It was, in fact, only Teresa's evident nervousness that had alerted him to what he was doing, enabling him to stop himself.

Looking at her now, glowing and alluring, he felt himself begin to harden with desire. But he must not. He could not.

He noticed that Teresa had suddenly flushed a deep red. He followed her eyes to see Lord Byron, who, with his good friend Scrope Davies, had limped over to her group in order to meet the newest sensation of the season. Warning bells immediately went off in Richard's head, and he quickly made an excuse to Lady Margaret to extract himself from the dance.

At Lady Cowper's drawing room Richard had once heard Teresa speak of her contempt for Byron. He had warned her then not to speak ill of the famed poet, as many people of the *ton* worshipped him, and she would only harm herself if she voiced her true opinion of him.

Now, hurrying over to her side, with Lady Margaret following disconsolately in his wake, he hoped that he was not too late to avert a disaster.

"Lord Byron, how nice to see you," Richard said smoothly. "Do you know Lady Margaret?"

Byron bowed to the confused girl on Richard's arm.

"I had thought to meet the newest marvel, Merrick. Your wife, I believe?" Byron drawled.

"Yes, and she is, indeed, a marvel. May I introduce you?" Richard moved closer to Teresa, whose color had resumed its normal hue.

"Lord Southerner was kind enough to introduce us already." Byron gestured to the large gentleman who was also a frequent attendee of Lady Cowper's drawing rooms.

"Unfortunately, he also felt it incumbent to relate one of Lady Merrick's more amusing comments regarding myself. Lady Merrick, am I correct in assuming that you had not actually intended for this to come to my ears?" Lord Byron smiled in a rather unpleasant manner at Teresa.

"Y-y-yes, my lord. I . . . I mean no, my lord. I had not intended for you to hear it," Teresa managed to say.

Richard scowled at Southerner. Although the gentleman was quite skilled at argument, and could be a staunch ally in Parliament, he was not well known for his use of tact.

Turning back to Byron, Richard smiled his broadest smile. "What Southerner does not know, my lord, is how much time my wife spends poring over your books, reading them and rereading them for the sheer pleasure of your wit and insight. Is that not right, my dear?"

Teresa eyes widened for a moment at the outright lie he was fabricating. But quickly, she caught on to the fact that Byron was practically preening with conceit at the thought of having his work so admired.

Her voice regained its strength, and she smiled sweetly at the poet. "Oh, indeed, my lord. Why, I am sure that I will soon need to replace my copy of *Childe Harold*. The binding is completely falling apart by being read so many times."

"No need, my lady, I will be more than happy to send you another copy, complete with a dedication on the flyleaf," Lord Byron said, running his hand through his carefully tousled curls and showing them his aristocratic profile.

"Oh, my lord, you are too good," Teresa exclaimed. "Please do not go to such trouble for me. I was planning on going to Hatchard's bookshop tomorrow anyway."

"Indeed? And may I ask what were you planning on purchasing there?"

"Er." Teresa's eyes narrowed in thought for a moment.

"Why, some new music, of course. There is a piece by Mozart I have been wanting to get."

"Mozart! My Lord Merrick, you allow your wife to play the music of Mozart? I have heard that it is quite beyond what is acceptable for a delicately bred girl." Lord Southerner was aghast.

Byron, however, found the idea that a proper English lady would play the music of such a well-known philanderer extremely funny. He slapped Richard on the back. "Excellent, Merrick, I applaud your forward thinking."

Richard had no choice but to try to appease them both. "Of course, Southerner, my wife may play whatever music she wishes at home. I do not know that it would be appropriate for her to play it in public, however."

Southerner seemed mollified by this, and went off to seek some refreshment. And Byron found that he was being hailed by Lady Jersey from across the ballroom and went off to seek other entertainment. As the group melted away, Teresa and Richard were left on their own for the first time all evening.

"Thank you, Richard, for twice saving my skin," Teresa whispered.

Richard smiled at his wife, warmed by the knowledge that his little bird was not quite ready to fly on her own.

Without a thought, Richard ran his thumb down her soft white cheek, his mind going back once more to his entirely improper thoughts of taking advantage of the fact that he was her husband. Let their agreement be damned, he wanted her.

Engrossed in his wife's charms, and his own increasingly vivid thoughts, he did not notice Doña Isabella's approach.

"Ah, the eager lovers," she chuckled.

Teresa's face turned red, and Richard felt his own face heat as well.

"M-M-Mama, please!" Teresa said.

"What, you are newly married. It is natural, *querida.*"

"What is natural?" Teresa asked.

"Why, for your husband to . . ." Doña Isabella stopped speaking and looked closely at her daughter. She then looked to Richard, her eyes wide. Her eyes darted down for a moment, and then a slow smile crept onto her face.

Richard felt his face heat even more and, too late, he crossed his hands in front of himself.

"An experienced woman knows, Merrick," Teresa's mother said, narrowing her eyes suggestively.

"Mama, what are you saying?" Teresa was completely confused. It was clear that she had no idea what her mother was suggesting or what she had seen.

Doña Isabella stepped closer to Richard as Lord Stowe and Lord Elybank joined them. Soon, members of Teresa's court, and not a few of his own, once again surrounded them. For once, the doña stayed quiet and allowed others to talk, but Richard noticed that her eyes kept slipping over toward him.

Within a few minutes he found her close to his side.

"Teresa is completely lost among your friends, is she not?" Doña Isabella said, tilting her head and looking up at him.

"Actually, Doña, most of them are *her* admirers, not mine," Richard replied, enjoying the look of confusion and surprise that greeted this news.

The moment did not last long. Doña Isabella turned toward her daughter. "*Querida,* why do you insist on wearing such awful colors?" she asked loud enough for all to hear.

Teresa turned a fiery red, which did not detract from

the lovely rose-pink of her elegant gown. "Mama," she said, "I . . . I like this color. Aunt Catherine picked it out for me."

"Clearly, your aunt has exceptional taste," Lord Stowe said.

This remark was seconded by quite a few of the other men present.

Doña Isabella drew her perfectly arched eyebrows down as she looked at Lord Stowe. He, however, was oblivious of her disapproving look.

She turned back to her daughter. "I will take you shopping, *querida,* and get you some clothes that flatter you. You are entirely too thin."

Richard was about to intervene, when Lord Stowe spoke up again.

"Is it difficult to have a dress made just right for such a lithe and delicate figure such as yours, Lady Merrick?"

"Er, no, not really, my lord." Teresa was clearly very embarrassed. Biting her lip, she looked around as if searching for something to distract her mother and Lord Stowe from their verbal sparring.

Once again Richard was about to step in to her rescue, but she took the initiative herself.

"My lords, do you all know my mother, Doña Isabella?" Teresa asked in a desperate attempt to turn her mother's attention away from herself.

The ploy worked almost better than Teresa had intended. Seeing the distinguished group of men turning toward her, Doña Isabella smiled and turned on her charm. Within moments, half the men had deserted Teresa in favor of her mother.

Silently, Richard applauded Teresa on her management of Doña Isabella. She clearly knew just what to do to distract her.

Richard turned to see Teresa surrounded by a whole new group of beaux. Where did they come from all of a sudden? he wondered. Well, he was certainly not just going to stand by and watch his wife being feted. He stepped in to join the crowd around her and heard Lord Hawksmoor ask, "Lady Merrick, is it true you play the music of Mozart?"

"Yes, indeed, my lord, a more gifted musician there never was. I have heard that he is brilliant in all that he does," Teresa said ingenuously.

The men around her all laughed, and some of the women tittered at Teresa's unintended *double entendre*. *Poor girl,* Richard thought sympathetically, *she has no idea what she just said. I'll just have to teach her.* He chuckled to himself.

The orchestra struck up the beginning chords of the supper waltz. Gentlemen requesting the honor of dancing with her and then escorting her in to dine suddenly surrounded Teresa.

Blushing slightly, Teresa looked shyly at all of the men. "I am so sorry, gentlemen, but I have promised this dance to my husband."

Ignoring the disappointed cries of the other men, Richard bowed low over her hand. He knew that his face was covered with a stupid grin, but he did not care. Teresa was his wife; he was very proud of her and thrilled that she had chosen him over anyone else.

Doña Isabella looked stunning. This fact caused Richard some discomfort since she was not only in his private library, but they were entirely alone.

After spending most of the morning going over the household budget for his orphanage, he had finally taken a break from the dreary accounts. Leaning back in his chair and massaging his temples, he had soaked in the comforting environs of his sanctum.

His large mahogany desk dominated one quarter of the room near the front window. Richly bound volumes lined two whole walls, and an ornately carved fireplace with a painting of Julia hanging over the mantel dominated a third wall. As he looked at the picture, his eyes had strayed, as always, to the white Aubusson carpet, which still showed the faded wine stain from the day that Julia had died.

"My lord, Doña Isabella is—"

"*Gracias,* Samuel, I told you I do not need to be announced." Trailing perfume that was unmistakably French, and unmistakably expensive, Doña Isabella had slipped into the room, closing the door firmly behind her.

Richard raised an eyebrow as he stood up. "Doña, what a pleasant surprise," he said smoothly. "Unfortunately, Teresa is not here at the moment."

"Yes. We will make the best of it." Doña Isabella smiled at Richard.

It was then that he fully noticed her appearance. Her low-cut crimson dress clung softly to her curving figure, showing just enough for Richard's mind to imagine what was underneath. And as always, he was amazed at how young she looked. There was hardly a hint of wrinkles around her beautiful blue eyes or her full red lips.

She made a great show of looking around his study. Then she walked slowly up to the desk where he was still standing, giving him plenty of time to admire her.

Carelessly, she pushed Richard's papers aside and sat down on the edge of the desk next to him. Ill-at-ease at her proximity, Richard picked up his work and tried to put it into an organized pile away from his mother-in-law.

"You have a very nice library, Merrick. Very masculine," Doña Isabella said slowly.

"Thank you, it is where I feel most comfortable."

"Mmmm, yes. I also like that you are very comfortable in society. We are very similar, no?"

"Well, yes, I suppose. Like you, I have always been a rather social creature."

"I like English society, and I have always enjoyed Englishmen. And English soldiers . . . they are such charming company. In Spain, I hosted them frequently."

"Teresa told me you held drawing rooms for them."

"Yes. Poor Teresa, she never enjoyed their company, unlike me. She was always rather . . . shy." She shook her head regretfully. "I would surround my daughter with attractive, eligible men and she would either be tongue-tied or would begin to stammer. She never knew what to say to them." Doña Isabella lowered her eyes and then looked up at Richard through her long black lashes. "She never appreciated men, like I do."

Richard found himself being drawn to her. She was so soft and feminine, so alluring.

"You can always tell what a man is like by the things he surrounds himself with," she said softly. She ran her hand across the desk, leaning forward so that Richard had a very clear view down the neckline of her dress.

He could not help but admire the unmistakable charms of the voluptuous woman before him. She was quite unique.

"Your English wood, it is so smooth and hard," she said, gazing at him with a calculated frankness.

Smiling at her innuendo, he decided to parry in kind. "Surely Spanish wood has the same qualities, but perhaps not quite the same . . . durability?"

Doña Isabella laughed a deep throaty laugh. "Hmmm . . . perhaps. Have you ever been to Spain, Merrick?"

"No, I haven't. It is very warm there, I suppose."

"Not only is the weather warm, the people there are hot-blooded as well. Not like many of the English." Doña Isabella looked at Richard intently, and then edged closer to him across the desk. "You are hot-blooded, Merrick, like me, no? You are not like the typical Englishman, like perhaps my daughter is—cold, frigid."

Doña Isabella's hand had begun to run up Richard's chest, slipping under his coat.

Richard's amusement faded abruptly as he grabbed her hand to stop its progress. Their flirting had been enjoyable, but now she was going beyond the limits of what was acceptable behavior. Enough was enough. Doña Isabella was an extremely enticing, sensuous woman, but he could not forget that he was married, and, moreover, married to her daughter!

"Doña, I think perhaps you should await Teresa in the drawing room," he said in his most stern baritone, returning her hand to her.

He had almost lost control of the situation, but he would make sure that it did not get out of hand. He had never had a woman be so forward who was not one of the demimonde. The fact that it was his own mother-in-law made the situation even more ridiculous.

Doña Isabella moved her body closer to Richard's, smiling suggestively up at him.

"But I would like to get to know you better. We are still such strangers, Merrick, or may I call you Merry?" Her voice was so soft that Richard was forced to move his head closer to hear her.

"You may, but only because you are like a mother to me." He smiled as a momentary expression of unease flitted across her face. Her confident look returned, however, as she stood up and took another step nearer him.

"Oh, no, I am like no mother you have ever had, Merry. And I want you to have me."

With her fingers she traced the line of Richard's chin. And at the same time he felt the unmistakable pressure of her soft hips against him.

Richard tried to back away, but he was trapped between his chair, which pressed against the windowsill, and his desk. His only recourse was to physically move the woman in front of him. He had gently taken her by the shoulders to move her backward, when his worst fear came to life.

Teresa walked in.

Eighteen

"Teresa, this is not what you think." Richard's hands dropped from Doña Isabella's shoulders as if they were scorched.

Teresa did not spare him more than a blank stare. "Mother, may I speak to you in the drawing room, please?"

She turned and left the room, not pausing or even turning around to see if her mother was following her.

Firmly closing the door to the drawing room, she turned to face Doña Isabella. "Mother, you may not play your games with Richard."

Teresa did not try to mask her feelings. She could barely believe how angry she was. Luckily, her anger was lending her bravado, and she was going to use every ounce of it to tell her mother exactly how she felt.

"Games? What games are you speaking of, *querida*?" her mother asked innocently.

Teresa was not fooled, not for one moment. "You know very well, Mother. Do not try to deny it. I saw you. I saw the way you were looking at him. I saw the way you were standing there, touching him."

Teresa had begun to pace furiously back and forth. She now stopped and stood still, glaring at her mother. It took a great deal of self-control to contain her anger, to keep her voice steady and low.

Her mother gave an uncomfortable little laugh. "We were just having a little fun. There was really nothing going on."

"Have your fun with someone else," Teresa said slowly in a clipped voice.

"But, *querida,* Merry is so enjoyable. I take pleasure in speaking with him."

"Flirting with him is what you mean to say," Teresa interrupted.

Her mother conceded the point. "All right, flirting with him. He is amusing. I do not mean anything by it, you know that." Her mother reached out to touch her shoulder, but Teresa moved out of her reach.

"I do not know that. Mother, I will say this only once more. Use your wiles on someone else. Leave Richard alone."

"Oh, but he is so . . . so masculine, so powerful. . . ."

"And my husband!" Teresa was now beginning to lose her tenuous hold on her self-control.

Teresa saw her mother's expression change subtly from a mixture of mischief and guilt to a rueful sadness.

"Querida," Doña Isabella said, "if he were truly your husband, I would not have touched him, I assure you. The fact of the matter is, he is *not* your husband."

"What do you mean?" Teresa was incredulous.

"He is not your husband until you consummate your marriage."

Teresa felt her face heat with embarrassment. How had her mother found out that she and Richard had a marriage in name only? Had he told her? Had he been the one to encourage her attentions?

No, she could not believe that of him. He lied, she knew. He disappeared constantly and probably could not be counted upon. But he would not have told any-

one, least of all her mother, about their agreement. She
was sure of this.

"How do you know?" Teresa asked, as much to herself as to her mother.

Her mother had sat down on the sofa. She leaned
back and made herself comfortable. "I am a woman of
the world, *querida*. I can tell when a man needs a
woman, and I have never seen a man more in need than
Merry. Honestly, *mi amor,* I want only to help you—and
Merry. And if you are not going to sleep with him, well
. . . someone must ease his desires."

The seriousness in her mother's voice, as much as her
words, stopped Teresa. She thought about this as she
slowly walked over to the sofa and sat down next to her
mother.

Teresa supposed she was right. But she wanted it to
be herself, not Doña Isabella, who sated her husband's
desires. "Why? And why must it be you?"

"It need not be me, *querida*. It should be you. As you
say, he is your husband."

Teresa swallowed hard. "And I want to be Richard's
wife." Her voice came out as a whisper.

"Then you must consummate your marriage." Her
mother said it in such a matter-of-fact way, as if there
were nothing to it. Teresa nearly laughed.

"Teresa, do you love him?"

Doña Isabella's question caught Teresa off guard. She
looked at her mother and thought about Richard and her
feelings for him. For so long she had tried *not* to think
about how she felt, perhaps even denying the fact that
what she felt for him was growing.

No one, least of all herself, had asked her that question. Did she love Richard? She could deny it no longer.
She did love him.

Then, all at once, Teresa felt like jumping up and

clapping her hands. Her heart felt light and she felt happier than she had ever been in her life. She was in love.

And yet, she also felt like crying. Yes, she was in love, but with a man who did not love her and probably never would. It was unrequited love, and that hurt more than anything.

And then there was her mother, who only a few minutes earlier had been running her hands up Richard's chest and flirting with him outrageously. Would Doña Isabella ridicule her or try to steal him away from her if she admitted the truth? Would she tell her that she had no hope of ever securing Richard's love in return? It was probably true, but it would hurt just the same to hear her mother say it.

"I think he is the most wonderful man I know," she said, deliberately not revealing her true emotions.

Her mother looked at her sideways, and Teresa could tell that she knew that her daughter was not telling her everything. She had always been bad at lying to her mother, but at least now she was not stammering.

"Then I say again, Teresa, you must bring him to your bed. It is the only way you are going to maintain your marriage. Otherwise, there is nothing to stop him from seeking out other women. It is only a matter of time, *querida*."

Teresa could not stand the idea of Richard being with another woman. Just the thought of it made her stomach tighten into knots. Very reluctantly, she agreed with her mother. "But I do not know how, Mama."

Her mother's eyes narrowed and her mouth curved up into that secret smile that had so confused Teresa the night before her wedding.

"You must take the initiative. You must be the one to seduce him. To entice him to your bed. He will come willingly, I am sure."

Teresa was flooded with anxiety. "But how? How could I possibly do such a thing? I do not know the first thing about . . . about that."

"Oh, you do not need to lead the lovemaking. You simply need to bring Merry to the point where he won't be able to stop himself. He will take over, and you will know what to do." Doña Isabella smiled slowly again. "You are my daughter, after all."

Teresa swallowed hard. No, there was no way she could do this.

"Teresa, do not worry overmuch. Men love it when women take the initiative. Why, I do not believe your father ever initiated our lovemaking."

"Mama! I . . . I do not think I should hear about . . . about you and Papa."

"Really, Teresa, do not be so high in the instep. Your father and I loved each other very much and we had a wonderful life together—in bed and out of it." Doña Isabella paused. "He was perhaps not quite as passionate as I would have liked. But then, I am a very passionate woman."

She smiled at her daughter and took her hand in a reassuring manner. "You need to discover whether you have inherited your passion from me or from your father. If it is from me, you will have no problem bringing your Merry to your bed. If it is from your father, well, then you must try harder to overcome it. But remember, *querida,* if you do not entice Merry to your bed and make him consummate your marriage, you will have to live with the love lost."

Teresa tried to perch on the arm of Richard's chair. The pose effectively showed off her ankles, she thought to herself, but it was extremely uncomfortable.

As she leaned closer to him, she inhaled his very masculine scent. As always, he smelled of his bay rum, but she had not smelled it at such proximity for some time. It made her senses reel.

Richard gave her a funny smile, as if he were trying to figure out what she was doing. Ignoring his look, she smiled at him in what, she hoped, was an enticing manner, and then swung her leg to emphasize her bared ankle.

She knew what she was doing was incredibly bold, but she also knew that her mother had been right. It was the only way to save her marriage, and now she knew for sure that this marriage was what was best for both her and Richard.

The past few weeks had taught her that perhaps Richard had been correct when he told her that she was attractive. Oh, she knew she was not beautiful like her mother, or as witty and charming as her, but surely there was something there that she had that attracted members of the opposite sex. Otherwise gentlemen at the Debenhams' ball would not have surrounded her. And if that were the case, then there was no reason Richard would not also feel that same attraction.

Richard raised an eyebrow and then stood and moved away. "I don't mean to take that chair if you would rather sit in it," he said much too politely.

"Oh! Ah, no. I just wanted to be closer to hear what you were saying," Teresa lied, and then slipped off the arm of the chair. Luckily, she caught herself before she fell onto the floor. But, she thought ruefully, it was not an elegant move and certainly not seductive.

Richard's lips twitched. "But I wasn't saying anything."

"Were you not just telling me about Fungy's horse?" Teresa asked.

"No. I finished telling you about that about five minutes ago, before we came to the drawing room," Richard said, looking at her oddly before turning to pour himself a drink.

"Oh." Teresa bit her lip. She had not meant for him to find out that she wasn't paying any attention to what he was saying. She had been too desperately busy trying to think of ways to entice him.

She wished her mother had been more explicit in her instructions rather than simply telling Teresa that she needed to bring him to the point where he could not stop himself. But how did she get him started?

Despite watching her mother for years, Teresa could not recall anything in particular that she had done to attract gentlemen.

Perhaps it was her décolletage?

Teresa pulled her dress down as low as it would go. But then she looked down at her distinct lack of cleavage. She simply did not have the curves her mother had. She leaned over to see if that would help.

"Are you all right?" Richard asked.

Teresa looked up, suddenly aware that he was watching her. She straightened quickly, and cleared her throat to stifle a sudden fit of giggles. She knew she was being ridiculous.

"Yes. I, ah, I thought . . . ah, I thought I lost my earring on the floor, but it is here." She fingered her earlobe, where her pearl earring was firmly secured. That was quick thinking, she thought with relief.

"You have been acting oddly all evening, Teresa. Are you sure you are not still upset over this afternoon?" he said, sitting down on a different chair, farther away from her.

"No, I assure you. My mother and I discussed it, and

she has promised not to . . . ah, not to do that again," Teresa finished awkwardly.

Richard nodded, although he still looked skeptical.

"I trust you, Richard, honestly I do. I know you would never . . . er, behave inappropriately with my mother." Oh, dear! The problem was that she had also trusted him not to take advantage of her either. And now she wanted him to.

Teresa looked over at her husband. He had his usual melancholy expression on his face. Now that she thought about it, the only time he actually looked happy was when they were out at a party. But that, she was sure, was simply an act, a face that he put on for society. She was glad he felt comfortable enough with her that he did not put on the act with her, but she also wished that he were happier. Perhaps it was as her mother said, he just needed some love and someone to love in return. Teresa squared her shoulders—she was going to be that person.

Teresa searched in her mind for something, anything, she could do to entice him. Richard had kissed her only once before, she thought with chagrin. How was she to get him to kiss her again?

Inspiration struck. Of course, the pianoforte. He had kissed her at the pianoforte.

"Richard, would you like me to play for you? The pianoforte, I mean," she said.

Her husband stood up rather quickly. "Yes, that sounds like an excellent idea."

Richard sat in his usual seat next to her at the instrument. She moved her chair a little closer to his and began to play a soft sonata by Haydn. But as she played, she deliberately transposed the music to a higher key so that she would have to lean across him to play the notes.

He moved his chair farther to the right so that she

could reach the keys she needed. Smiling to herself, she stopped playing momentarily to move her own chair closer to his.

Now he could not reach to turn the page of music without leaning across her. But that would have disrupted her playing, so, instead, he stood up and moved to her other side.

Teresa frowned. She was stymied once again and beginning to feel overly embarrassed by her forward behavior. It was a fun game, but it was clear that that was all it was going to be, a game. And now with Richard standing on her left and well away from her, what could she do?

She stopped playing.

"I . . . I think I am tired. I am going to go to bed if you do not mind, Richard." She hoped he would follow her up to her room as he had the other night.

He looked confused but a little relieved. "All right. Good night, then."

"Good night." Teresa stood and moved toward the door, but her husband did not follow her. "Are—aren't you going to come upstairs?"

"No. It is still early. Perhaps I'll go out to my club. I believe Fungy, Huntley, and Reath said they would be there this evening."

"Oh." Deflated, Teresa realized that her initial attempt at seduction had been an abject failure. But there was nothing more she could do. "Good night," she said again, and then slowly walked up the stairs to her room.

What had she done wrong? She had completely embarrassed herself all evening by bending over him, getting so close she could feel the heat of his body and smell his scent. Surely, if he was at all interested in her, these tricks would have elicited some response from him.

A laugh escaped from her, causing her maid, who was helping her to undress, to look at her oddly. Teresa bit her lip to keep the rest of her laughter inside. She could barely believe how ridiculous this whole evening had been. She had been reduced to chasing her reluctant husband around the piano in an absurd game of tag. And the expression on his face when she slipped off the arm of his chair . . .

What a fool she had been.

She was glad that she was laughing, because otherwise, Teresa was sure that she would be crying.

Nineteen

Richard watched Doña Isabella talking to her daughter quietly in the opposite corner of the room. All the guests from Teresa's dinner party had left except for Lady Swinborne, Lord Stowe, and his mother-in-law.

The evening had been an eye-opening experience for Richard. He had learned that his new wife was an excellent hostess, creating a warm and welcoming atmosphere for the few guests they had decided would be necessary to invite. The evening had gone remarkably well, and Richard had not had to do anything himself beyond simply showing up and playing the congenial host.

He had also discovered throughout the course of the evening that there was something beyond a platonic friendship between Doña Isabella and Stowe. Their behavior, while strictly circumspect, had nevertheless led him to this conclusion, and he knew that Teresa had been completely oblivious of it. They had shared the looks and small touches of those who knew each other intimately. Suspecting that his wife had hopes in Stowe's direction, he wondered what she would do once she found out that he was not going to be available for her to marry after they had had their marriage annulled.

Well, it was a problem that could be put off for another day. At the moment Richard was becoming more and more uncomfortable with the expression on his wife's face. She looked very upset with whatever her mother was telling her.

He watched for a few moments, debating whether he should intervene or not. Somehow, it looked like Doña Isabella was lecturing her daughter or explaining something to her, but it wasn't something that Teresa was happy with. This was evident in her heightened color and the way she kept shaking her head.

Finally, Doña Isabella laughed and said in a louder voice, "*Querida,* either take my advice or not, it is up to you." She then gave her daughter a kiss and said good night. Stowe had offered to walk both Doña Isabella and Lady Swinborne home, so the three left together.

Teresa looked oddly at Richard, her color becoming more intense.

"R-R-Richard, I am going to retire," she managed to say.

Richard felt terrible. Whatever it was her mother had said to her, she was clearly still upset by it. His heart weighed heavily in his chest. He desperately wanted to make her feel better, to protect her from her mother's harsh words, to do anything he could to help her.

He gave her arm a bracing squeeze. "Of course, my dear. It has been an exhausting day for you."

She did not look consoled at all. Instead, she was looking at him oddly, as if trying to figure something out. She reached some sort of conclusion.

Turning her head slightly, she looked up at him from beneath her long black eyelashes and gave him a slightly hesitant smile.

Richard was startled. It was almost the same look her mother had given him the other day when she had been flirting with him.

When given that look by Doña Isabella, it had made

his blood warm. But when Teresa did it, he boiled. Suddenly, his mouth was very dry and his palms were wet with sweat. He could not fathom why Teresa was doing this, but as he watched her look coyly down at the floor and then up at him once again, he was sure that this time her attempts at flirtation were definitely working.

"Richard, perhaps . . . perhaps you could help me. My maid was feeling ill earlier this evening, so I told her to go to bed early. Do you . . . do you think you could come up and help me with my buttons?" Teresa's voice was soft and low.

The room had become much too warm, and Richard found himself smiling and nodding. "Of course, I would be happy to help." All of his good intentions to stay true to his promise not to touch his wife flew out the window. He could no more stop himself from following her than he could stop a runaway post chaise and four.

Inside her bedroom, only one candle was lit, creating flickering shadows that danced on the walls and floor.

He closed the door behind him and then stood, unable to move, as he watched Teresa at her dressing table slowly pulling a few pins from her hair. The blue-black tresses fell in thick waves down to her waist as she gave her head a little shake.

Without noticing that he had even moved, Richard saw his own hand approaching her hair. He ran his fingers through the silky softness that slipped and curled around his wrist.

Teresa's large black eyes were looking up at him. She seemed a little scared, but had tilted her head toward his hand, accepting his caress. Her pale white skin seemed almost luminescent in the semidarkness. He ran his thumb down her soft cheek and over her pink lips.

Slowly, she turned around and moved her hair so that he could undo the buttons down the back of her dress.

His hands shook as he slipped each tiny pearl button one by one out of its loop.

He wanted this more than he had thought possible. He needed this woman, and his need rendered him deaf to the calls for sanity that whispered in the back of his mind.

Ever so slowly, her dress opened to reveal more of her white skin and the top of her corset. As he undid the last button, her dress slipped almost silently to the floor, with only the slightest rustle of silk as she stepped out of it and even closer to him. He took a small step back and began to untie her corset for her. All of the laces opened, and she allowed that to slip down to the floor as well.

Teresa turned around and moved her hair back, revealing her small breasts, which showed clearly through her thin cotton shift. He reached out to touch her and heard her sharp intake of breath as his finger ran over the sensitive flesh.

He was without thought now. All he knew was the beautiful, nearly naked woman before him. The soft glow of the candle behind her was effectively making her white shift transparent.

He leaned closer and inhaled her subtle lavender scent. She smelled so good. His lips gently touched hers. She was warm and trembled ever so slightly. Delicately, treating her as if she were a china doll, he enveloped her in his embrace, deepening his kiss as he pulled her closer in his arms.

Her mouth was sweet as she opened herself to him. He drew a ragged breath and let go of her for an instant to quickly divest himself of his coat and waistcoat. He didn't want to hurt her delicate skin with his buttons, but before she could say anything she was back in his arms, his lips once again pressed to hers.

Feeling only his intense need for this woman to be

his, entirely his, he backed her up until her knees pressed against the side of the bed. Once again he managed to remove his clothing quickly, without interrupting her lovely sweet kisses. His desire was overwhelming everything else.

Soon he was next to her on the bed, touching her naked body with his hands. He simply could not get enough of her. He had to touch every inch of her, he had to taste her, smell her. He even pressed his ear to her chest so that he could hear the rapid heartbeat inside of her. She made no other sound, but accepted his caresses and tentatively reached out to touch him as well.

As she ran her hand ever so lightly along his chest, her fingers caught in his hair. Gentle fingertips glided lightly over his nipples, and he thought he would explode right then and there. He swallowed hard and controlled himself, but when she allowed her hand to slide down to his abdomen and below, he could stand it no longer. His blood was pounding in his ears, but he forced himself to remain calm and to proceed slowly.

He moved on top of her, feeling with his fingers that she was ready for him. With the greatest amount of control he could manage, he slid inside of her. A small part of his mind registered that she was still a virgin, and he needed to be careful.

He heard her sharply suck in her breath. Softly, he cooed soothing words in her ear, but he knew that he would not be able to continue moving slowly for much longer. Already his body was demanding more.

He held his breath. He did not want to scare her, or to hurt her any more than was necessary. He could feel the trembling throughout her body. He moved as gently as he could, holding his breath in an effort to maintain his tenuous control over himself and his own desires.

Her startled cry lasted for only a moment, but then the

tension was relieved. He continued his movements, this time murmuring words of encouragement in her ear.

Once again he felt her tension build, but now it was good, pleasurable tension. He did all he could to heighten her pleasure. But finally, he could not hold himself back any longer. With a cry of satisfaction he let himself go, feeling her waves of pleasure rippling around him as she, too, experienced the ecstasy.

His breathing slowed, but he could still feel her heart pounding beneath him. He ran tiny kisses up her neck, over her pounding pulse, and to her ear. A feeling of deep satisfaction settled happily somewhere inside him.

Tentatively, she kissed his earlobe, and then he heard her voice. So soft, even quieter than a whisper, just a breath that said, "Richard, I love you."

He pushed himself up to look her in the eye. Had he heard right?

Teresa looked up at him. Her large black eyes sparkled in the dim candlelight, her hair was spread out like black silk across the pillow. And then she said it again. "I love you, Richard."

Teresa had never experienced such a feeling of completion—of being one with someone else. Making love with Richard had been all she had ever dreamed of, all she had ever hoped for. Her love for him was overflowing and she had voiced it. And now he was moving away from her. She felt bereft, empty.

"No, Teresa. You do not. You are mistaken." His voice sounded hollow as he stood and moved away from the bed.

She sat up and looked at him, and at the shadows flickering over his beautifully naked body. "But I do." She was confused. Had he not just made the most wonderful love to her? Didn't that mean that he loved her too?

"No, you do not. You cannot." And then he was gone.

Teresa could hear thumping in his room and supposed that he was pulling out clothes for himself. And then there was the final bang of his bedroom door, followed less than a minute later by the deeper thud of the front door being slammed shut.

Then silence.

Teresa curled up on her bed. There were no tears, there was nothing but emptiness.

Had anyone ever been so wrong? It amazed her. How could she have been so thoroughly and absolutely wrong? Wrong in what she had done and wrong in what she had thought.

Teresa lay there for some time but could not sleep. She got up to put on her nightdress and a wrap, and then took her candle and went downstairs.

After wandering about the quiet, empty house, she found herself outside Richard's library. Out of curiosity, she went in. She had been in this room only once before, and then only momentarily, though her husband spent a lot of time there. Perhaps it would make her feel better, almost as if he were there and hadn't just stormed out of the house in anger and frustration.

She raised her candle, looking around at all the books lining the walls. What a wonderful way to surround yourself, she thought. No wonder he loved this room. The light spread slowly as she walked around looking at random book titles. And then her light fell on the portrait above the fireplace.

Teresa stopped and stared, holding her candle higher so she could see better. The young woman in the painting was lovely. With a smile on her face and laughter in her eyes, she looked almost lovingly down from her frame. By her dress, Teresa figured the painting could not have been done more than a year or two ago. This had to be Julia.

Again, Teresa did not wonder why her husband spent so much time in this room. She was here. Julia was here with him all the time. In this room, in his house, and in his heart.

All of her tears and heartache burst forth in a torrent. She could not deny it any longer. Her husband was still deeply in love with his first wife. Her candle nearly dropped from her hand as she fell to the floor, her legs unable to support her any longer. She set the candle aside and wept into her hands. How could he have married her, no, insisted on marrying her, when he was still so much in love with Julia. Did he not realize the pain and suffering it would cause both of them? She held nothing back now, but let weeks of fear, heartache, and loneliness pour out of her.

How long she sat there sobbing, she did not know. But it seemed like hours. Her head hurt from the tension of crying for so long. Her heart hurt from the pain of her discovery and her husband's rejection after making love to her.

Her breathing finally calmed and she sat rubbing her temples to try to ease the pain there. There was nothing, she knew, that would ease the pain in her heart.

A red wine stain on the carpet next to her caught her attention. She stared at it for a full minute. She did not know why, but she hated that stain. She had to do something about it. It galvanized her like nothing else could, and she knew that she was being completely irrational. But for the next hour or more she scrubbed at that stain, using every method she had ever learned to remove stains. Her tears mixed with cornstarch, mixed with lemon, mixed with everything she could think of to get rid of the stain. By daybreak it was gone, and the carpet was once again white.

It was almost too white in that one spot, but the stain was gone.

Twenty

Richard walked the streets aimlessly before unconsciously making his way to the rookeries. In his current mood, the filth and squalor he found there seemed more comfortable than the neat and opulent homes of Mayfair.

The smell of rotting debris assailed Richard's nose. Fleet Street, just beyond the dingy streets of Drury Lane and Covent Garden, was teeming with a nightlife beyond anything Richard had imagined. Even in his more wild bachelor days, he had not ventured into this area at night for fear of footpads or worse. He had heard that many young bucks would frequent these East End pubs for fun, but always in a group.

Children who should have been tucked safe in bed were left sleeping on the streets while their mothers solicited the attentions of gentlemen passersby. Their fathers, if they even knew who they were, were too busy getting drunk in the tavern or fighting on the street corner to pay them any mind. If they were lucky, Richard supposed, someone was out robbing one of the city swells in order to get money to buy them some food to fill their empty bellies.

After just having fallen prey to his own baser instincts, he felt no better than any of the craven thieves and half-wits who lived here.

He shrugged off the grasp of a female who reeked of gin. She leaned close to him and grinned, her blackened teeth and foul breath making him recoil. She lowered her dress and shoved her bare breast at him, trying to entice him to purchase her services for the evening, but Richard had had enough of that.

He could not understand how he had allowed himself to get so caught up in the web of Teresa's innocence and his own desire.

How could he have betrayed Julia like that? He loved Julia. How could he have made love to another woman? How could he have defiled Julia's memory in that way? He had made a mockery of his marriage vows to her.

He looked at the woman still trying to get his attention, and felt his stomach turn. He didn't know which disgusted him more, the woman or himself.

He moved on through the blackness of the streets. With the waning moon being the only source of light, it was easy to see how thieves were able to escape so easily into the dark, winding streets.

In daylight these streets were familiar to Richard. It was from here that he had culled his boys to fill his orphanage. He knew he had only skimmed the surface of the rookeries for the few boys he had rescued, but the reality of the night haunted him.

If only he had not ignored the warning bells that had sounded in his mind when he had entered Teresa's room. If only he had kept his word to Julia and to Teresa, he would not be here. He would be safe, alone, in his own bed—filled with desire, he knew, but that was better than being filled with remorse and disgust at himself, as he was now.

His mind strayed back to Teresa. What had he done to that poor girl? He had consummated their marriage after promising her he would not. He had let his desires overpower his reason and common sense.

He had ruined her life and bound her to him without recourse, without the possibility of a second chance. There was nothing he could do now.

He did not love her, but she, innocent that she was, had somehow convinced herself that she loved him.

How could that be? How had she fallen in love with him when he had avoided her at every opportunity, being with her only when it was absolutely necessary? He had left her alone for hours every day while he sought refuge in his own orphanage or at his club, or had locked himself away in his library. Julia would never have put up with his absences as Teresa had. But his new wife had never known anything else from him.

And yet he had felt his desire for Teresa grow. He dared not even think that it might be anything more than that. He would not allow his mind even to contemplate any deeper feelings for Teresa.

No, he loved Julia. He loved her with all his heart and his mind. There was no room for Teresa in his life.

And yet Julia had left him. She had left him without a word—killed suddenly and inexplicably. How could she have done that to him when he loved her so intensely? He kicked at a pile of garbage, sending the debris flying along the gutter and a pig snorting after it.

As he walked along the line of the houses to avoid a brawl that had stumbled out of a tavern, he saw a shadow. A boy, probably not older than four or five, fast asleep, curled up in a doorway. He was beautiful, with the most angelic little face. It was much too thin, Richard could see that right away. Such a face should have been round and chubby, but this little one was so skinny, it made Richard's heart go out to him.

Sitting down by the side of the building, he gently

lifted the boy into his lap, cradling him, lending him his warmth. The boy stirred and then opened his large eyes to stare up at him.

"Do you know where your mother is?" Richard asked gently.

The little boy nodded. "She's in 'eaven."

Richard blinked rapidly for a moment. "And your dad?"

"Don't 'ave one," the boy whispered, looking like he was about to cry.

Richard hugged the child close. "Then I'll take you someplace safe, away from here. Would you like to live with lots of other boys who are all like you? Where there are people to care for you?"

The little eyes went wide. "Is it 'eaven? Will I see my mummy?"

Richard's voice caught, and he was unable to speak for a moment. "No. It's not heaven. It's just a nice house where you can live," he managed to say through the lump in his throat.

"Oh. I s'pose so." The boy shrugged and sounded a bit disappointed.

Richard stood up with the boy still in his arms, unwilling to let go of his little burden, receiving as much comfort from the child as he hoped he was giving. The boy put his arms around his neck and rested his head on his shoulder as Richard walked to his orphanage.

It took a few minutes for someone to answer his pounding at the door. The footman who finally answered looked barely awake. Richard requested some hot water and then took the boy down to the kitchen to bathe him in front of the fire.

He was impressed, as the child did not utter a sound while he was bathed and dressed in a clean nightshirt. Somehow Richard took solace in the simple act of caring for this child, in scrubbing away the filth and grime that encrusted his little hands and feet and in washing his hair, which turned out to be a dark blond, like his own. He then took him upstairs to the last empty bed in the room for younger boys.

It was only when he went to put the child into bed that boy started to shake and then to cry. He clung to Richard's neck, refusing to let go.

"No. Ye promised ye would take care o' me," the little voice wailed.

"Not I. I promised you there would be others to take care of you, and there are. I promise you. It is only because it is the middle of the night and they are all asleep. You will see. There are lots of maids and footmen, tutors and a very kind and loving headmistress, Mrs. Long. She will take care of you."

"But I don't want no one else. I want ye. Don't leave me!"

Richard clung to the little boy, knowing just what he felt like. He hadn't wanted Julia to leave him either, but she had. And he had to leave this little one. At least he knew that he would be well cared for. And he, Richard, could come back.

"If I promise to return tomorrow, will you let me go?"

"Y' promise?" the boy hiccoughed.

"Yes. I promise. I will be back tomorrow to check on you. I come every day to check on all the boys here."

The boy sniffled and then wiped his nose on his sleeve. "Awright, if ye promise."

"I do." Richard tucked the child into bed and then went down to the drawing room to write Mrs. Long a note.

When Teresa awoke late the following morning, the events of the previous night returned to her like a lead weight. Still, she managed to get herself up and dressed. Then she continued to do what she had started last night in a small way. She began to clean.

Donning an apron, she organized the servants in a grand spring cleaning of the entire house. From the attics to the basement, everything was to be turned out and cleaned thoroughly. Every room except his lordship's library.

Teresa had learned from the housekeeper that Richard was there, and had ordered his breakfast brought in to him on a tray. At midafternoon it was the same thing. He still had not come out, and it didn't look as if he was going to. Which is why Teresa was so surprised, when she finally sat down for a brief rest later that afternoon, to learn that his lordship had gone out. But by dinnertime he had returned to his library and was once again requesting that his meal be taken in there.

The pattern was repeated on the following day. Richard rose early and was in his library when Teresa came down for breakfast. He was still there when she stopped her cleaning to take luncheon, but then disappeared for a few hours later in the day. At dinner he was returned and still requested his meals to be taken in to him.

On the evening of the third day, Teresa toyed with the idea of knocking on his door to speak with him, but she did not know what to say. Should she apologize? How could one apologize for loving someone? Teresa left him alone.

After nearly a full week of doing nothing but cleaning, Teresa was physically and emotionally exhausted, and Richard still had not shown himself. Somehow, he slipped out of the house every afternoon, unnoticed by all, only to return to take his dinner in his library.

She knew he came out at night to sleep in his bed, but

only because the upstairs maid had said that his bed had, in fact, been slept in. No one had seen him, however, not even his valet. That gentleman had reported that his lordship's razor had been used, clothes left in a heap on the floor and fresh ones removed from his clothespress, but he had not been present when his lordship had been there.

He was like a ghost living in the house. Everyone knew he was there, but no one ever actually caught a glimpse of him except for the butler who delivered his food.

Teresa could not help but think that it was her presence there that was keeping him locked up as he was. She supposed that he would much rather be with Julia in the comfort of his library, but to shun everything else so completely was a little disturbing.

She briefly wondered where he went every afternoon. She knew it was not to his club, for Fungy had called one day when Richard was out and said that he had not been seen.

Teresa did the only thing she could think of to help him—she left.

After seeing to the packing of her clothing into a trunk, Teresa wrote Richard a note to be delivered to him if he asked after her. She tried to keep her tears from falling on the paper, but in the end, the ink was rather smeared. She did not attempt to write it again.

In the note she explained that she was moving back in with her aunt. She knew it probably was not far enough away to be of comfort to him, but it was her only option. She prayed for his happiness and that perhaps, someday, he might find it in his heart to forgive her for hurting him in this way. And she signed it simply "Teresa." She had thought to write "your loving wife" but decided that would upset him even more, so she had simply written her name. She gave the note to the housekeeper and then, with one last look at the closed door to Richard's library, and her throat choked with emotion, she left.

The quiet of the house caught Richard's attention. For so many days there had been a constant low level of noise, which had seemed to come from every corner of the house. He had no idea of what was going on and did not particularly care to. He had shut himself up in order to hide from the pain, just as he had done after Julia had died.

He had lost a little of his spirit after his mother and sister had died in their carriage accident, and then again when he had learned of his brother's death in the war. But when Julia had died, it seemed as if all of the life had gone out of him. A little returned each time he went to the orphanage, and he continued to go there even now. It was his only living tie to Julia.

Teresa had forced him to truly live his life for a little while. But now he felt just as he had after Julia had left him, and he still could not face Teresa.

It was the sudden silence of the house, however, that was disturbing him now.

Very tentatively, he opened the door of his library and peered out into the entrance hall. His footman was there, standing silently like a statue, staring straight ahead.

Richard went into the dining room, and found another footman quietly polishing the gleaming wood of the table. Upstairs in the drawing room a maid was going about dusting a spotless room. She, too, was absolutely silent.

It seemed as if everything was normal. The servants

were there doing their jobs. They were just so quiet, and everything, Richard noticed, was oddly clean and shining. All of the wood smelled of fresh beeswax; all of the silver gleamed like it never had before. He could not remember his house ever being so very clean.

But there was something missing. Richard could feel it under his skin. Something was wrong.

He went down into the kitchen, where even the cook was working wordlessly, preparing dinner. He found Mrs. MacPherson in her sitting room, silently going over household accounts.

She looked up, startled, as he came into the room. "Och! M'lord, I dinna hear ye coom in."

"That is surprising, considering how quiet everything is. Why is that, Mrs. MacPherson?"

"Why is what, m'lord?"

"Why is everyone so quiet?" he asked again.

"I dinna know fer sure, m'lord," the housekeeper answered, as if she might be holding something back.

"Mrs. MacPherson?"

"Aye, m'lord?" The lady began to smooth down her apron in a nervous way.

"What is going on?"

She went over to her cupboard and took out a note. Handing it to him, she said, "Perhaps this'll answer yer question, m'lord."

Richard took the note and recognized Teresa's handwriting. And then it hit him. That was what was missing! Teresa!

"Where is Lady Merrick?" he asked the woman standing in front of him, still looking very uncomfortable.

"I s'pose that'll tell ye, m'lord. She left it with me were ye to ask after her."

Richard nodded brusquely, figuring that this was all

he was going to get out of the woman. He went back upstairs, opening the letter as he went. In his study he drew
back the curtains for the first time in over a week, needing the light to read the note. Settling himself in his
favorite chair, he read through the few lines of the note
twice, and then stared into the empty fireplace.

She was sorry for what *she* had done to *him*? What
had she done? He was the one at fault. He had been the
one who had let his desires overpower his common
sense. She had only followed her misguided heart.

And now she had left him. Just like Julia. Teresa had
left him.

When had she done this? He looked for the date and
noticed it was two days past. He shook his head in
amazement. He had not known. He had been so caught
up in his own frustrations and guilt that he had not even
noticed until today that something was not right.

The smudged letters bespoke of her sadness as she
had written the letter. Richard dropped his head into his
hands. How could he have let things go so far?

A beam of sunlight caught his attention. Following
the light, he looked down to the carpet near his chair
and onto a spot that somehow looked whiter, cleaner
than the rest of the carpet around it. Richard stared at it
for some time with an odd feeling in his chest.

Was it just the sunlight or was that spot truly whiter?

And then it hit him like a blow to his gut. Where was
the wine stain? The wine stain that had become a part
of his carpet on the day Julia had died. It was gone. It
had been right where the beam of sunlight now shone.

He got down on his knees on the carpet, feeling it
with his hands, as if his eyes were somehow deceiving
him and only by touching it could he be certain that it
was real. But it was real. The carpet felt oddly stiff just

in that spot, as if a little of whatever had been used to clean it had been left there.

He ran out of the room. Completely forgetting about the bell system he had had installed so many years before, he called at the top of his lungs for Mrs. MacPherson.

The woman came panting up the stairs, running toward him. "What is it, m'lord? What's wrong?"

"Mrs. MacPherson, what has happened to my carpet?" he demanded, pointing into his study.

The woman looked at him oddly, and then went into the room. Looking about the floor, she shook her head. "I dinna know what ye're talkin' about, m'lord. Nothin's happened to yon carpet."

Richard strode over to the spot where the sun still shone. "There, Mrs. MacPherson, there. Where is the wine stain that has been there for over a year?"

The housekeeper followed him and looked down at the spot. "Och, that one. Well, ye know, m'lord, I've been scrubbin' at that stain off and on ever since it happened. I've never been able to get it up, but Lady Merrick, she said she got it up. Worked at it all night, I believe she said. Told me so when we was doin' our spring cleanin', m'lord."

"Your spring cleaning? When did you do spring cleaning?"

"Why, we've done nothin' else for the past week, m'lord. The mistress said we wasn't to disturb ye in here. And she had already gotten the wine stain out anyway."

Richard felt oddly out of place. He did not know what had been happening under his own roof, and he had been there all the while.

"When did she do that, did she say?" Richard asked, but somehow he already knew the answer.

"Must have been a week ago Friday, m'lord," the

housekeeper said, still a bit confused over her master's intense questioning over one little stain.

Richard nodded. The night they had consummated their marriage. She had probably come down here to find him. But what had she found instead? He looked up at the picture of Julia hanging above the mantel and then down at the spot on the carpet just in front of it. Slowly things were beginning to come together in his mind.

"Thank you, Mrs. MacPherson."

The housekeeper bobbed a curtsy and then left him alone.

Richard looked at the carpet one more time and then up at Julia. As always, she was looking down at him with laughter in her eyes and a smile on her face, but this time it truly looked like she was laughing at him.

And well she should, Richard thought to himself. He had been a fool. He had found someone who truly made him happy, who had made him want to live again, and then he had driven her away.

Yes, reluctantly, he admitted it to himself, Teresa made him happy.

He sat down in his chair. He missed her. He missed hearing her play the pianoforte. He missed having funny conversations with her about silly enormous horses and wine fountains in the shape of the sphinx. He missed her sense of humor and her intelligence. The way she glowed when she played her music and the way her face lit up and her eyes became intense when she argued for the returned soldiers. He missed her presence in his home.

He looked up at the painting. "I will always love you, Julia. But Teresa makes me want to live again. I cannot live without her. Tell me, Julia, tell me that it is all right to live again."

He stopped and waited. He wasn't sure what he was waiting for—lightning to strike him down? Julia's painted smile to fade? But there was nothing.

And then he heard it. The ticking of the clock on his mantel. He listened harder. There was the sound of birds chirping in the trees just outside his window. Carriages were rolling past, their horses clopping quickly down the street. A fruit seller was crying out his wares—apples, oranges, and luscious berries. A woman was selling flowers; he could hear her song as it harmonized with the fruit seller's.

The sounds of life. So ordinary and yet so beautiful to someone who had shut himself off from it for so long. But he would do so no longer. He wanted to live, and he wanted to live with Teresa.

Without further thought he ran out the front door of his house, and a moment later he was pounding on the door of Lady Swinborne's house next door.

Twenty-one

Teresa was startled but not too surprised when she emerged from the breakfast parlor to find Lord Stowe sitting with her mother in the drawing room.

She was used to her mother having men visiting her at all times of the day. And despite the fact that her mother had buried her father only three months earlier, she knew that to ask her mother to live without a man would be like asking a fish to live without water. It simply could not be done.

She had thought, nevertheless, that Lord Stowe would behave with more propriety. But then, he had also come to call at an odd hour the day before. Perhaps, Teresa thought wryly, it was the effect that her mother had on the men around her—one of those knowing half-smiles, and propriety was the last thing on the minds of her beaux.

"Good morning, Mama. Lord Stowe, what a pleasant surprise to see you here so early," Teresa said mildly, trying to hide her curiosity.

"Good morning, Lady Merrick," Lord Stowe said, his ears turning red with embarrassment as he hastily stood up from the settee he had been sharing with her mother. At least *he* realized that his presence at this time of day was not what was strictly proper, Teresa thought.

"Good morning, *querida,*" her mother said with a smile. "You are looking charming this morning."

Teresa stopped mid-stride and looked at her mother. Was Doña Isabella, in the presence of a man, actually complimenting her on her appearance? But then, her mother had been unusually pleasant, even kind, recently. Why, Teresa had been completely floored the previous evening after dinner when her mother had said that she was proud of the way Teresa had blossomed over the past few months since she had been here in London.

But that was a comment made in private. Teresa's experience had always been that her mother had saved her most scathing and disparaging remarks for when they were in company, especially the company of men.

Teresa looked speculatively at her mother, but all she got in return was her usual dazzling smile. Doña Isabella patted the settee next to her, where Lord Stowe had vacated his seat.

Teresa sat down as her mother asked, "Have you any plans today, Teresa? Perhaps—" She looked frankly at her daughter. "Perhaps you will see if that husband of yours has emerged yet from the refuge of his library?"

Teresa had told her mother the whole of what had happened, and now she was very sorry that she had. She had not been allowed to hear about anything else for nearly two days—ever since she had returned to her aunt's house.

"No, Mama. When Richard is ready to come out, I'm sure that we'll hear of it through the servants. Until then, there is nothing more that I can do."

Teresa braced herself for the flood of rebuke that was inevitable. Instead, there was an awkward silence for a moment, and she thought she saw Lord Stowe and her mother exchange a little glance.

"*Querida* . . ." Doña Isabella began.

"Yes?" Teresa turned to her mother. There was clearly something going on, but she had not the faintest idea what it could be. Looking at Doña Isabella's beautiful face, Teresa realized that she had never seen her look so uncomfortable. She had a small frown between her eyes, and yet underneath it she seemed oddly calm, even serene, with none of her usual nervous energy.

"Harry—er, Lord Stowe, that is—has asked me to marry him," Doña Isabella said slowly, not looking at her daughter but instead over at Lord Stowe, who was still looking rather flushed. "And I have accepted."

"He has? You . . . you have?" Teresa's mouth nearly fell open as she struggled with her thoughts. But seeing how her mother was looking at Lord Stowe and that the look was reciprocated, she realized that she should not be surprised at all. Now that she thought about it, her mother and Lord Stowe had been together very frequently of late.

She tried to gather her wits together. "Well, that is wonderful. Please accept my warmest felicitations."

"Thank you, Teresa," her mother said, but her words were reflexive, as her eyes did not move from those of her newly betrothed. Stowe, for his part, also seemed caught in the spell and, uncharacteristically, did not respond to her words of congratulation.

Teresa rose from her seat, still struggling to understand the deep ache she now felt in her heart. Was she disappointed at this turn of events? After all, she had, at one point, thought that she might be interested in Lord Stowe herself. He was charming, handsome, with a raffish air lent by his eye patch—yet kind and thoughtful. He was everything she had thought she would want in a husband.

"I will leave the two of you together," she said, moving toward the door. She got no answer, as her mother and Lord Stowe seemed to have forgotten that she was even there.

Looking at them, she realized that the ache she felt had nothing to do with the fact that her mother had been the one to win Lord Stowe's affections. No, the more she thought about it, the happier she was for them.

Lord Stowe, who was so kind and good, deserved every happiness that was coming to him. And her mother needed a man not only to keep her company but to fill her heart.

Leaning against the closed door to the drawing room, Teresa knew that her heavy heart was not due to Lord Stowe's having found his soul mate. It was because she had found her own . . . and then lost him forever, locked behind the solid wooden door of the library in the house next door.

The warmth of the sun that afternoon was almost too much. Teresa was tempted to retreat into the cool of the house, but it was too quiet there. Lord Stowe had left after he and her mother had informed her aunt of their good news, and then the two ladies had gone out to pay their morning calls, leaving Teresa alone. Oppressed by the silence in the house, she had come outside to the garden.

It would have been so pleasant if it were not for the heat. The air was as fresh as it could be in the city, and there was the singing of birds and the chatter of some squirrels in addition to the normal noise of everyday life.

Teresa leaned back on the bench that was perfectly placed out of the sun. The shade of the lone tree of her aunt's tiny garden provided, at least, some respite from the heat.

She wondered whether Richard had yet noticed that she had left, or if he was still hiding himself away in his library with Julia.

A tear slipped down her cheek. It was hard enough that her husband didn't love her, but that it was his dead wife whom he loved over her made it so much more difficult. She couldn't compete with a dead woman.

She brushed away a second tear but missed the third one. Squeezing her eyes shut, she tried to stop feeling sorry for herself.

The sound of muffled footsteps in the grass distracted her, and then she felt someone sit down on the bench by her side. Teresa opened her eyes.

Richard was next to her.

Teresa shook her head in disbelief. He was here. Richard had finally come. The tears began to flow again. She didn't know what to say or what to do.

He looked awful. His blond hair, which he had cut short to be more in tune with the current style, was standing at odd angles, and his face somehow looked older, with more lines around his tired eyes. His neckcloth was untied, and his waistcoat and coat were both unbuttoned, as if he hadn't had the time or energy to dress himself properly.

He handed her his handkerchief but then took her hand so that she could not use it.

"Please, Teresa, do not cry."

His voice was soft and comforting. Taking a deep breath, she made more of an effort to stop herself.

"Teresa, I want you to come home."

Teresa felt her breath catch and looked up at her husband. He wanted her to move back to his house? Why? Was it pride or social ridicule that he was worried about? Or something else entirely? She tried to discern what it was by looking into his eyes, but she could see nothing there. He seemed just as closed off to her as he had been before.

"Why?"

"You are my wife," he answered simply.

So it was pride. Well, she had pride, too, and she was not going to go running back to him the minute he called. She knew that he did not love her. Why should she go back to him and live in a loveless marriage? Teresa sat up straighter.

"No, Richard. There is nothing for me there. There is no reason for me to return."

Richard took a deep breath. "I am there."

"No, you are not! You are never there! I never see you," she said, her pain taking refuge in a burst of anger.

"I spend every single evening with you. Is that not enough?"

"No. It is not enough. Why do I never see you during the day as well?"

"I . . . That was not part of our agreement." He moved away from her by a fraction of an inch, as much as the space on the bench allowed.

There was something else that he was going to say, Teresa was sure of it. There was something he was not telling her.

"I promised to make you a social success and I have—and at no little cost to myself, I might add," he said, his voice deepening.

"What do you mean?" Teresa was suddenly confused. What could making her a social success cost him?

"I mean that it was not easy for me. To be social." He stopped speaking and looked down at his hands that were interlaced on his lap.

"But you are the Merry Marquis. You have always been a part of society."

Richard shook his head. "No, Teresa. I *was* the Merry

Marquis. I am no longer. Without Julia it is just an act. I cannot be merry without her."

Teresa stopped to think about all the parties they had been to. He had been merry—most of the time. But then again, there had been times when he wasn't or when it was too forced. And then there were the few times when they were attending a party and he had disappeared altogether for half an hour or more. She did not know where he went, but now she realized that perhaps he had gone someplace to be by himself because he could not maintain his facade. And she had known that it was a facade and had been happy when he did not try to be that way with her when they were alone.

"I . . . I hadn't realized . . . I did not know," she said, feeling awful that she had not understood how difficult it had been for him. She had not fully realized all that Julia had been to him. It was no wonder that he still loved her and missed her as much as he did.

"Yes, well, now you do." He looked directly into her eyes, as if challenging her to mock him or perhaps, even worse, feel sorry for him.

"Then why did you do it? Why did you take me to all those parties?"

"Because I promised that I would allow you to meet other men, to find a husband you could love and who loved you. And I promised to save your reputation." Richard shrugged. A half-smile played on his lips for a moment. "You needed me and you needed the Merry Marquis."

"So you did it for me? Even though it was so difficult for you?" Teresa was touched. She reached out and put her hand on his. "Thank you, Richard." He may not love her, but he was true to his word, and he was a good friend.

He covered her hand with his other one. "I will always be there for you when you need me, Teresa—if you come back."

It was a small touch, but it filled Teresa with a warmth, a feeling so good, she wanted to do nothing more than sit there like this, holding his hand.

She knew that Richard was not offering her his love. He had none to give her, but he was offering his friendship and support.

She wanted so much to be with him, but could she accept living with him on his terms? Teresa thought about this, and then thought about her alternatives. She could stay here, with her aunt, as she supposed her mother would be moving elsewhere after she and Lord Stowe were married. Either way, she could still try to find a man who loved her, as had been her original intention. But she would always love Richard.

That made up her mind. She would accept what he could offer and be happy with that, for it was the most she would get, and perhaps in time . . .

"Yes, Richard. I will live with you."

He released his breath and gave her hand a squeeze, clearly relieved and happy with her decision.

There was still one thing that bothered her, however. "Richard, where *do* you go? During the day. Is there someone . . . someone else? Do you have a mistress, perhaps?" She stopped, and then asked as gently as she could, "Or do you go to her grave?" There was no need to explain whose grave she meant, and the knot in her stomach tightened at the thought. She didn't want to hurt him, but she had to know.

The smile faded from his face. "No. Julia is buried in the family plot at Merrick in Wales. And no, I do not have a mistress to whom I go. Perhaps I should have, but what is done is done."

Teresa was not sure she understood that last part. Was

he referring to their lovemaking? She supposed he was sorry that he had allowed himself to become intimate with her. This hurt even more than the thought that he was still in love with his dead wife.

Richard looked uncertain for a moment but then said, "If you want, I will take you to the place I go every day. In fact, I would like you to come and see it. Perhaps then you will understand."

Now he was truly talking in riddles. Teresa had no idea what he meant. Where was he going to take her?

A smile had slowly spread across Richard's face. He stood up and took her hand. "Teresa, come with me."

The brass plaque outside the building proclaimed it to be "The Merrick Home for Destitute Boys." Teresa stopped and stared at the plain facade of the house. It was an ordinary enough house, perhaps bigger than those all around it and located just across from a large expanse of park.

Inside it was warm and friendly. Paintings of green countryside, horses, and farms were hung on the walls of the hallway and the drawing room.

The drawing room was clearly decorated with children in mind, Teresa noted. There were no fragile ceramic pieces decorating the tables, but instead sturdy, overstuffed sofas and chairs, creating a homely atmosphere where a child or children could relax and feel comfortable.

Mrs. Long, the headmistress, greeted Richard with familiarity and Teresa with some surprise.

"The boys are at their lessons now, as you know, m'lord," she said a little apologetically.

"Yes, thank you. I think I will just give Lady Merrick a tour of the house."

"Very good, sir." Mrs. Long curtsied and then left them alone.

"We have twenty-five boys living here, Teresa," Richard explained, leading her down the hallway toward the back of the house. "They were all found living on the streets of the rookeries."

"Found by whom?" Teresa interrupted.

Richard stopped walking. "By me. I used to walk around the streets beyond Drury Lane."

"But is that not very dangerous?"

"Only if I were to go about in clothes such as this," he said, pointing to his very fashionable, if rumpled, coat of blue superfine and buff-colored pantaloons. "But I have old clothes that I wear when I go out, so that I blend in better."

"That is what you were wearing when I first met you."

Richard smiled, and looked a bit sheepish. "Yes. You always came to practice just as I returned from my for-ays into the rookeries."

They continued down the hall.

"We have a full-time staff residing in the house, in-cluding seven footmen, five maids, and Mrs. Long, of course. There are two full-time tutors who come every day and two part-time tutors to assist with the morning lessons. It took me the longest time to find just the right people to fill all these positions, since a great deal of pa-tience is needed to deal with the boys' antics."

They stopped outside a classroom and peered in through the open door. The room had two long tables, around which sat ten boys, five at each. The tutor, who was standing in the front of the room, stopped his les-son when he saw his lordship come in with a guest. Teresa supposed the boys to be between the ages of nine and twelve, as they stood and bowed to her and Richard.

"Gentlemen, I would like you to meet my wife, Lady Merrick," Richard said.

In one voice the boys all said, " 'Ow do you do, ma'am."

Richard went around each table naming each child for her. She was impressed, and not a little surprised, that Richard knew them all by name.

"What excellent manners they have, my lord. I am very impressed." She smiled at the boys, who broke into smiles and a few giggles.

"I should hope so. I have tutored them myself. The older boys and I take tea together every day," he explained.

"You do?" Teresa was stunned. So that explained where he disappeared to every afternoon. Things were really beginning to come together for her.

They left the boys to return to their lesson.

"Why did you not tell me about your orphanage before?" Teresa asked, stopping Richard in the hall with a touch of her hand on his arm.

He turned to her and looked deeply into her eyes before answering. Shrugging, he said, "Most people of the *ton* would look down on me for taking an active role in the running of an orphanage, or any other charity, for that matter. If one must engage in charitable activity, it should be done at a distance. That I have dirtied my hands by actually running the institution myself would horrify quite a few people. Honestly, Teresa, I did not know how you would react if you knew."

Teresa was hurt.

"But you know that I believe very strongly in taking an active role in helping others. Did I not spend most of my childhood entertaining the British soldiers in Spain? Do I not now spend much of my time trying to find ways to help those same soldiers who have returned, destitute, to England? How could I think any less of you because you are helping these poor children? No, I am not like the rest of the *ton,* Richard, you should know that."

A smile lit up his eyes, and Richard reached out and stroked Teresa's cheek with his thumb. "I do know that now. It is one of the many things I admire about you." He suddenly noticed his hand on her face and pulled it away as if it were burnt.

"Come and meet the younger boys," he said, turning away, but not before Teresa noticed that his color was slightly heightened.

She supposed he was embarrassed at his show of affection. She also wondered if she wasn't blushing too, since her cheek was still hot from where he had touched it.

Richard led the way into the next room, which was not quite so orderly as the first. Two young men were attempting to teach the alphabet to fifteen boys ranging in age from four to eight. However, as soon as Richard took one step into the room, any attempt at following the lesson was quickly forgotten as all the boys ran screaming enthusiastically toward him.

Teresa realized her mouth was open in amazement at the reception her husband was receiving.

Richard squatted in order to accept hugs from the younger boys. A few of the older ones held back, but Richard reached out and ruffled their heads affectionately.

She found herself blinking rapidly to try to hide the tears that had sprung to her eyes at the open display of love and affection from these children. That he spent quite a bit of time here was obvious from the fact that they were all so at ease with him.

The little ones were trying to climb onto his knees,

while older ones were putting their hands on his shoulders and clutching at his arms. All of them were trying to gain his attention and all were talking at once. Richard was smiling and laughing at what one boy was telling him, while kissing the hurt finger of one of the youngest ones. He gently reprimanded an older child for pushing another and made a vain attempt at giving each boy some of his attention.

One thing was very clear to Teresa as she stood back and watched—Richard was going to be a wonderful father. The love and attention he gave to these boys was incredible.

Her heart suddenly filled with a longing that she had never felt before. Would she ever have children of her own?

And if so, would they be Richard's? Her stomach tied itself up into knots. She felt herself wishing more than anything that they would be his, but at the same time, she thought it rather unlikely. The gulf that stood between them, and the lack of love he felt for her, made it an impossibility. At the thought, she had to restrain herself from running from the room in tears.

She held her breath and tried to wipe her eyes surreptitiously, but one beautiful little blond child came up and gave a tug on her dress. "Are you cryin', lady?"

She knelt down to his level. "Yes, I am a little. And do you know why?"

"No, why?"

"Because I am so happy to meet you and all of the other boys here. Do you like living here? Is it a nice place?"

"Oh, yes! It's the most wunnerful place in the world!" came a very enthusiastic response.

"Good. And what about his lordship? Is he kind to you? Do you see him often?"

"Govna? 'E's the best! 'E comes and plays wif us ev'ry day."

"Does he? That is very good of him. I am happy that he does so."

And she truly was. No longer did she need to wonder where Richard went every afternoon. Nor did she feel bad that he wasn't with her. He went where he was needed most.

Guilt stabbed at her for accusing him of going to Julia's grave or having a mistress. His reasons for leaving her alone were entirely altruistic. He had important work to do here, and she was glad that he did it. She wished she could find some way to apologize or take back her harsh words.

Teresa noticed that Richard had managed to extract himself from the crowd of boys, and accepted his hand to help her stand up.

"Boys, you may all make your bow to Lady Merrick, and then back to your studies," he said in a kind but commanding voice.

There was a little grumbling, but all of them did as they were told.

As they walked back to the front of the house, Teresa could not hold back her admiration for what Richard had accomplished here. "It is fantastic, Richard, how you have given these boys a home. And it is clear that you and Mrs. Long take excellent care of them."

"Thank you. It has taken a lot of hard work to get this place to where it is today. I must admit that I am proud of the way it has turned out."

"You should be. And you should be proud of yourself as well. To give so much love and attention to these boys who need it most is truly a remarkable thing."

Richard looked uncomfortable at her praise, but Teresa was truly awed by what she had seen and what her husband had done. It was a rare man who could be so selfless and devote himself to those in need. To take children from the slums of the city and give them a home and love was wonderful.

And Richard had not been altruistic only in his orphanage. Teresa knew full well, now, just how difficult it had been for him to do all that he had done for her as well. He had put aside his own feelings of self-doubt and discomfort in order to help her overcome her own insecurities. He had pretended to be something he was not in order to make her comfortable in society.

She desperately wished that she could do something in return for him. She knew the one thing he would probably like most would be if she could bring Julia back to life. But she could not do that.

Perhaps she could try to do for him what Julia had done. Surely, Julia didn't have some magic power that had made Richard the Merry Marquis. He had been that way before he met her. Teresa had heard about his antics and how all the other young men would copy his lead. So what was it that Julia had done for him? Made him feel comfortable? Gave him self-confidence? She could do that.

He had already begun by himself to be the Merry Marquis. Even though he had said that it was an act, it should be easy to show him that it need not be. All he needed was the security to know that he could be himself.

If he could give her the confidence she needed to become a social success, why could she not do the same for him? Teresa was determined to do this for him.

When they reached home, Teresa gave orders to the footman to have her trunk brought back from her aunt's house, and then followed Richard up to the drawing room.

While he was pouring himself a drink, Teresa went directly to her little desk where she had kept all of their invitations. Searching through the pile of cards, she found exactly what she was looking for.

"We have an invitation tonight to Lady Wynworth's rout," she said, turning to Richard.

Teresa almost burst out laughing at the stricken expression that came over Richard's face. "Do not look like that, Richard. We had promised to attend."

"That is wonderful. I am sure that Fungy will be delighted to escort you," Richard said, turning away from her and walking to the door.

"Oh, no, Richard. I could not go with Fungy! Why, what would people say?" Teresa worried for a moment that her husband was going to try to back out of attending this party with her. If he did, the plan she had decided upon would not work. She could not help him if he did not come to the party. He had to come.

She gave him a pleading look. "Please, Richard."

Her husband frowned at her, one hand on the doorknob. "Did I not explain to you just a short while ago how difficult it has been for me to go to these parties? In any case, you don't need me anymore. You're a success, just as I had promised you would be."

"You did, Richard, you have done a fantastic job in making me so. But I am sorry, I would be completely lost without your reassuring presence. Fungy will not stay with me and help me in conversation as you do. I have grown quite dependent on knowing that you are there to help me out if I get myself into trouble."

Briefly, Teresa felt guilty about using Richard's own kindness against him. But it was for his own good, she reminded herself.

Richard paused and scowled at the doorknob in his

hand. "Very well," he finally conceded. "I will escort you, if I must."

"Thank you, Richard, I promise you'll not regret it." Before he could change his mind, Teresa raced out the door Richard held open for her.

Twenty-two

Teresa had never seen Richard so nervous before. He didn't show it in any obvious way, but Teresa could tell. Perhaps it was how he held himself, with his back so stiff. Or perhaps it was the smile that, though charming as ever, seemed painted onto his face and never reached his eyes. Whatever it was, she knew that he was uncomfortable.

She was not feeling entirely comfortable herself either. Not only had they not been to a party in a week, but now Teresa realized that she was the one who had to take the lead. Richard, she knew, was not going to have an easy time slipping into his merry self.

She looked around the room, trying to find likely people with whom she felt most comfortable. Since she was going to have to be outgoing and charming, she needed to be with friends.

She spotted Lord Millhaven and waved her fan in his direction. He was speaking with Lady Margaret, but at her beckoning, the two of them moved toward her and Richard.

"Good evening, Lady Merrick," Lord Millhaven said, taking her hand and placing a salute upon the back of it.

Richard was doing the same to Lady Margaret, who was looking quite dazzling in bright pink.

"You look lovely this evening, Lady Margaret," Richard said.

"You don't think me too bright, my lord?" Lady Margaret said, turning around for him to admire her dress.

"Oh, no, one could never accuse you of being too bright," Richard managed to say with a straight face.

Teresa choked on a laugh and succeeded in turning it into a small coughing fit. A thump on her back from Richard cleared it up, and she was able to share a look with him without losing control again. The twinkle in his eye boded well.

And poor Lady Margaret was always leaving herself open for such comments. Thankfully, she was completely oblivious of any implied insult.

With perfect equanimity Richard asked the lady to dance, leaving Lord Millhaven open to do the same with Teresa.

After a few dances with various ladies who simply presented themselves for the honor, Teresa could tell that Richard had begun to relax a little. She continued to stay close to his side when neither of them was dancing, as much for her own feelings of comfort as to support him.

She hoped she was being as charming and witty as she needed to be in order to allow Richard to show to his advantage. She was firm in her decision to make him be as at ease in his role among the *ton* as he had made her.

Teresa redoubled her efforts to be charming. She remembered how she had been able to win over Lord Stowe when she had put her mind to it, even though all the times she had done so it had been through anger at criticisms. Still, when she wanted to, she could be as captivating as her mother. She also tried to bring forward that feeling she got when she played the pianoforte. It allowed her to forget to be self-conscious. Bringing all these pieces together was the key, she realized, to her social success. Summoning up all the charm and wit she could, and combining that with her determination to be sparkling, she let herself loose.

Before she realized it, she had attracted quite a number of beaux to her side. And where the more eligible gentlemen were, the matchmaking mamas, with their daughters in tow, soon followed.

Teresa's conversation flowed; she laughed and even made daring witticisms. And she brought Richard along with her into this sparkling web she was weaving. He really had no choice. When the gentlemen flocked to her side, she made sure Richard was included in every conversation. When the ladies joined them, she redirected his attention to them.

But through it all, Teresa kept to Richard's side. She turned down dances when he wasn't dancing and always returned to him the moment a dance was over. He still was not completely relaxed, but she could tell he was making progress in the direction as the evening wore on.

There were still moments, however, when Teresa would catch him looking off at nothing. He would retreat into himself each time he had a moment's quiet.

She noticed that he was standing alone while she was dancing with Lord Riverton. She didn't know how he had come to be alone, since when she had been asked to dance he was engaged in a light banter with her mother and had two other young ladies and their mamas eagerly awaiting their turn to speak with him. As the dance ended, she looked around for her husband but could not find him anywhere.

Excusing herself, she went out onto the balcony, thinking he might have escaped there to be alone.

Her instincts had been right. She found him standing in a dark corner, leaning on the balustrade overlooking the garden.

"It is entirely too hot in that room!" she said, leaning her forearms next to his.

Through the pale light that filtered from the house behind them, she could just make out the curve of his lips as he smiled. "Indeed. Although the air is not much cooler out here, at least it is refreshing," Richard said, not moving or even looking over at her.

Teresa took a deep breath. "Yes, it is actually a lovely evening, is it not?"

Teresa peered at her husband in the dim light and was struck at how incredibly handsome he was. His taste in clothing was impeccable, as always, and the tired lines she had noticed around his eyes—was it only that morning?—had eased as he had begun to relax. Even when he was not animated, he still was the most handsome man at the party. She had missed him terribly when he had disappeared into his library. She was glad that she had agreed to live with him once again. It felt good just to be with him.

She wished she could reach over and take his hand, but she did not know if her touch would be repulsed or not. She was still too unsure of her position and how he felt about her. They stood next to each other, looking out at the dark garden in comfortable silence.

"There they are!" Reath's voice broke in on their quiet.

"Really, you two have made yourselves the talk of the party, hanging on each other's sleeves like young puppies. Embarrassing!" Fungy said as Richard's three closest friends joined them.

"At least Merry should know better. Teresa can be excused, as she is still so new to our society," Huntley agreed.

Richard raised his hands in mock surrender. "I claim innocence! I have not been hanging on my wife's sleeve, it is she who has been hanging on mine. Why, she hardly even has any sleeves," he said, picking at the small puff of fabric that graced Teresa's nearly bare shoulders.

Teresa hung her head but could not hide her smile. "I plead guilty. I am sorry if I am destroying Richard's reputation."

"Destroying it? No, indeed, you have been the making of his reputation. You complement him," said Huntley.

"Yes. That's it. Complement him. Couldn't think of the word," Fungy agreed.

"What do you mean?" Richard looked from one man to another.

"You and Julia were a pair, Merry. You were both witty and fashionable," Reath began. Teresa felt Richard next to her withdraw at the mention of Julia's name, but Reath either was unaware or deliberately ignored it.

"Indeed! Great pair. Just the same, you were. Two peas in a pod," Fungy drawled. But then he continued before anyone else could say anything. "Not Teresa though. Adds something new."

Reath turned to Fungy. Raising just one black, slashing eyebrow and frowning, he gave him a look that would have had Teresa shaking if he had turned it on her.

"Yes, as I was about to say before I was interrupted, Teresa complements your wit and air of distinction, Merry, by being quietly charming and clever."

"They truly are a great combination, Teresa's intellect and Merry's address," Huntley agreed. "Still, you know you shouldn't hang on each other, it's just not done."

Richard looked down at Teresa with a new appreciation in his eyes. "It may not be the done thing, but it is the comfortable thing. Without her here, I do not believe I could be quite so merry."

Teresa looked into Richard's eyes and felt her heart melt at the warmth she saw there. His thumb stroked her cheek ever so gently, sending shivers down her spine.

A discreet cough abruptly reminded her and Richard that they were not alone.

She was sure she flushed, because even Richard's face had turned slightly pink, but she turned back to Richard's friends. "Well, if we do not return to the party, people are certainly going to begin to talk."

She moved to take Richard's proffered arm, but then stopped and took Huntley's instead. "You did just say that I should not hang on my husband's sleeve," she reminded them all.

Amid laughter, they returned to the party.

Somehow, after that Richard was much more at ease. He finally allowed his true self to emerge. And his sparkling presence attracted as many admirers as Teresa's had earlier. She no longer had Richard's sleeve to hang upon, however, since it was almost constantly being occupied by other ladies. She did not mind this at all because it simply meant that Richard had come back into his own—he truly was the Merry Marquis.

She lost sight of Richard at some point but now had no worries about him. She was sure he was charming some lady off her feet.

Toward the end of the evening, Teresa noticed people putting their heads close together as a whisper of scandal spread quickly through the room.

She excused herself from the conversation she was having with the elderly Lord Kendal and moved to where Fungy and Reath were standing talking with Lady Jersey. Surely, if anyone were to know what was happening, it would be Lady Jersey and Fungy.

"What is the latest on-dit, Lady Jersey?" Teresa asked.

The lady looked uncertain for a moment, biting her lower lip.

Reath, however, had no qualms about sharing the gossip. "Merry is either being a complete idiot or is making an absolutely brilliant social move. We have yet to learn which way the wind will blow."

"Taken his social reputation and tossed it into the lap of Princess Lieven," Fungy added.

"It is a daring move for anyone who values their social standing," Lady Jersey said, nodding her head. "She has been known to destroy even the most secure leaders of society."

"Just a nod from her or a frown at the right moment, and all would be lost," said Fungy, beginning to look nervous.

"Indeed, Merry has made an exceptional comeback. To risk it all in this manner is simply foolhardy." Reath shook his head sadly.

Teresa felt her palms begin to sweat. She looked around desperately to see if she could spot her husband. Finally, by following the line of sight from others who were also watching Richard take his very social life into his hands, she found him.

He was standing and talking with Princess Lieven at the far end of the long, narrow room. Teresa could not make out whether the princess looked happy or not. If not, it would be the end of the Merry Marquis. But on the other hand, if he managed to charm her, it could very well set him at the pinnacle of society once again.

Teresa's heart leapt into her throat. It was one thing for Richard to be charming and witty when he was with her, Teresa thought, but for him to take it to the highest stickler of the *ton* entirely by himself was a leap of faith and the ultimate show of self-confidence. Teresa was both terrified of what might happen and more proud of her husband than she had ever thought possible.

As she watched, Richard took Princess Lieven's hand and bowed low over it. He leaned forward and whispered something in her ear. And then Teresa saw the most amazing response, the lady smiled and fluttered her fan. All the signals were there, she was charmed.

Teresa smiled and turned to Fungy. "He's done it. I knew he could."

But Fungy wasn't smiling. In fact, he was looking even more worried than before. The orchestra has just struck up a waltz.

"Bad luck!" Reath exclaimed vehemently.

Teresa turned back toward Richard and Princess Lieven. Biting her lip, she watched as Richard bowed low once again. The serious expression on the lady's face did not bode well. And when she lifted her chin up a notch as Richard said something else to her, Teresa was sure all was lost. But then, ever so slowly, she placed her hand in Richard's and allowed him to lead her out onto the dance floor.

Teresa remembered, once again, to breathe.

As they rode home, Richard could barely remember the last time he had felt so good. He had truly, for the first time since Julia had died, felt entirely comfortable in society.

He was back. He had put aside his mourning—thrown off the mantle of depression and loneliness that had engulfed him for the past year. He felt like his old self again.

He tried to peer through the darkness at his wife. She had done it. She was the one who had helped him do this. He was sure that if she had not been there for him, he would never have had the confidence to be himself.

Despite her own popularity, she had continued to stay by his side and support him. Throughout the entire evening he could turn to her, see her smiling faith in him, and get a spark of confidence in himself. Somehow she had neatly turned the tables on him, supporting him and his self-confidence instead of the other way around, as it had been before.

How could he have ever thought that he could live without her? Just knowing that she was always going to be there for him had helped him, had given him the confidence he needed.

She was so vital to him, and so beautiful as well. And best of all, she was his wife. The thought sent a warmth through his veins, and a pool of happiness settled somewhere deep inside him.

Silently, he reached across the carriage and took her hand. He knew that he should thank her for being there for him. But somehow he was sure that she understood, as her fingers intertwined with his.

Twenty-three

Richard heard the beautiful music and felt all his muscles relax. As he stepped into his house, the tension of having tea with ten wild young boys and attempting to teach them proper manners slipped from his shoulders.

The scent from the bouquet of lavender and roses, which graced the hall table, added to his sense of well-being as he stopped and listened.

The recently waxed wood floor reflected the sunlight that streamed in through a window overhead. Richard placed his hat on the table next to the flowers, and could not resist running his fingers delicately over one of the feathery fronds of the lavender, releasing even more of its lovely scent.

There was not a more beautiful sound in the world to Richard than Beethoven's Fourteenth Sonata. The soft, lilting melody, which used to remind Richard of Julia, now brought a picture of Teresa to his mind's eye. He could almost see her swaying to the beautiful music she created, her eyes half closed, her long black eyelashes delicately resting on her white cheeks.

He let the music lead him down the well-lit hallway to its source, but then paused with his hand on the knob of the music-room door.

The ghosts that had haunted him were gone. And in his heart he knew it was Teresa who had banished them.

There was now only brightness and light where once there were shadows. She had swept clean his morbid thoughts and made him want to live. It was Teresa who had brought light and love into his life once again.

Love. He did indeed love her. He knew this now.

But he had promised that theirs would be a marriage in name only, and that he would grant her an annulment when she found someone who loved her.

But *he* loved her. He could not allow her to have their marriage annulled. He could not allow that!

He was suddenly filled with anger at the thought of anyone else holding his sweet Teresa, of loving her as fiercely as he did.

Richard squared his shoulders and threw open the door. It flew open so hard that it banged against the opposite wall.

"Teresa, I cannot keep to our agreement."

Teresa was so startled by the sudden intrusion that she stood up quickly. The delicate gilt chair she had been sitting on fell backward with a loud crash.

"Richard! What is wrong? What are you talking about?"

Richard strode into the room and grabbed hold of Teresa's hands. "I mean that I cannot honor my word, my promise to you. If you ask for it, I will refuse to grant you an annulment from this marriage. I love you and I want you to be my wife now and forever. Tell me that you have not fallen in love."

Teresa smiled up at him, tears glistening in her eyes. "But I have." She paused.

Richard thought his heart had stopped for a moment as his mind raced.

Who was it? Millhaven, Corstairs?

Pain sliced through him. He could not bear to lose her again.

"I love *you,* Richard. I told you," Teresa said, looking up at him through her long black eyelashes.

His heart started pounding in his chest, bursting with joy.

And that look! She was regarding him with that seductive look that she had learned from her mother.

Richard could not resist her open invitation. He leaned forward and slowly lowered his head to hers. He kissed her sweet pink lips and drank in her beautiful lavender scent. He pressed her soft body to his and squeezed so tight, he heard her gasp.

"Richard, are *you* sure about this?" she managed to say when he loosened his grip.

"I have never been so certain of anything," he said before tasting her sweet lips once more.

But then he felt her stiffening ever so slightly in his arms. He pulled back and looked deeply into the dark pools of her eyes.

"And Julia?" she asked.

Filled with his love for her, he cradled her face with his hands. "Julia is gone, Teresa. You make me want to live. With you I can truly be myself once more. You have made me whole."

This time it was Teresa who moved first, pulling his head down to hers. He could feel her love flow into him through her kiss.

Richard found that he could barely restrain himself. He needed to touch her, to kiss and feel every inch of her beautiful, slender body. His desire for her was becoming palpable, and he could feel hers building for him in the way she pressed herself against him.

He could not wait even a moment longer, he had to show Teresa exactly how much he loved her. Richard swung her up into his arms. "Come live with me, Teresa, and be my wife."